CHARACTER ENCYCLOPEDIA

THE WHO'S WHO IN THE MARVEL UNIVERSE

Based on the writings of Steve Behling

Illustrated by:
Steve Kurth, Mike Huddleston, Geanes Holland, Michela Frare, Michela Cacciatore, Simone Boufantino, Carlos Barberi, Ario Anindito, George Duarte, Eduardo Mello, Dario Brizuela, Gaetano Petrigno, Cucca Vincenz, Salvatore Di Marco, Roberto DiSalvo, Angela Copolugo, Olga Lapaeva, Vita Efemova, Anna Beliashova, Tomasso Moscardini, Davide Mastrolonardo, Pierluigi Cosolino, Fabio Pacuilli, Guilla Priori, Ekaterina Myshalova, Nataliya Torretta, Stefani Renee and Caravan Studios

First published by Scholastic Australia in 2020.
This edition published by Scholastic Australia in 2023.

Scholastic Australia Pty Limited
PO Box 579 Gosford NSW 2250
ABN 11 000 614 577

www.scholastic.com.au

Part of the Scholastic Group
Sydney • Auckland • New York • Toronto • London • Mexico City • New Delhi
Hong Kong • Buenos Aires • Puerto Rico

ISBN 978-1-76129-127-2

Printed in China.

Scholastic Australia's policy, in association with its printers, is to use papers that are renewable and made efficiently from wood grown in responsibly managed forests, so as to minimise its environmental footprint.

CHARACTER ENCYCLOPEDIA

THE WHO'S WHO IN THE MARVEL UNIVERSE

SCHOLASTIC
SYDNEY AUCKLAND NEW YORK TORONTO LONDON MEXICO CITY
NEW DELHI HONG KONG BUENOS AIRES PUERTO RICO

CONTENTS

INTRODUCTION

You've heard of the Amazing Spider-Man, the Incredible Hulk and the Invincible Iron Man. You might even be able to list all the members of the Avengers, or know the name of Earth's current Sorcerer Supreme . . .

But do you know which Avenger is king of his own country? Or which villain has their own business in New York City? How about which Avenger trained in a circus as a kid? Or which hero is an android created by Ultron?

Find the answer to all these questions and more in this encyclopedia!

SPIDER-MAN & HIS FRIENDS

HEIGHT: 177 CM

WEIGHT: 81.6 KG

SUPERHUMAN STRENGTH

SUPERHUMAN AGILITY

SUPERHUMAN ENDURANCE

STICKING TO AND CLIMBING WALLS AND OTHER SURFACES

SELF-DESIGNED WEB-SHOOTERS, ALLOWING HIM TO FIRE AND SWING FROM STICKY WEBS

'SPIDER-SENSE' THAT WARNS OF INCOMING DANGER

GENIUS INTELLECT, SPECIALISING IN CHEMISTRY

SPIDER-MAN

Peter Parker

Hey! You! Person reading this book! Have you ever been bitten by a radioactive spider? No? Of course you haven't! That's not the sort of thing that happens every day. But it happened to Peter Parker!

Peter was just a regular teenager at Midtown High. He was a good student and science was his favourite subject. All that changed one day during an excursion to the Science Hall when a strange spider bit him and gave him incredible powers! He became super-strong and could stick to walls. He even had a 'spider-sense' that could warn him of danger!

But Peter didn't use his powers to help people at first . . .

At first, Peter wanted to make money and he had to find a job where he could use his powers to his advantage—so Peter became a wrestler. He used his strength to beat all his opponents.

One night, Peter noticed the wrestling gym was being robbed. But instead of stopping the robber, Peter turned a blind eye and let the robber get away.

Later that night, when Peter got home, the police told him and Aunt May that Uncle Ben had been viciously attacked! The police had tracked the criminal to an old warehouse. Peter knew he had to take matters into his own hands.

When he got to the warehouse and captured the crook, Peter realised it was the same man as the one who robbed the wrestling gym. Peter desperately wished he had stopped the thief and from then on, he vowed to use his new powers to make the world a safer place—starting with his own neighbourhood. So he made himself a cool costume and a pair of web-shooters. Now he fights crime as Spider-Man!

One day, Spidey was swinging through the boroughs of New York City. He was looking out for bad guys, and he was always sure to find one. Suddenly, his spider-sense went wild! Spidey saw one of his old foes—the Shocker! This guy wore bands on each hand that could cause super-strong vibrations. The vibrations were SO strong that he needed a costume with padding to help absorb the shocks. The suit made him look like a bed mattress. At least, that's what Spidey thought.

'Come back, Mattress Man!' Spidey called out. 'I wanna introduce you to some friends!'

'You'll have to catch meeeeee!' the Shocker said.

Now, the reason the Shocker said 'meeeeee' was because Spidey had just caught the bad guy in his web and yanked him back. Then he turned the Shocker over to the police.

All in a day's work for your friendly neighbourhood hero, Spider-Man!

HEIGHT: 165 CM

WEIGHT: 56.7 KG

SUPERHUMAN STRENGTH

SUPERHUMAN AGILITY

SUPERHUMAN ENDURANCE

STICKING TO AND CLIMBING WALLS AND OTHER SURFACES

MECHANICAL WEB-SHOOTERS, ALLOWING HER TO FIRE AND SWING FROM STICKY WEBS

'SPIDER-SENSE' THAT WARNS OF INCOMING DANGER

GHOST-SPIDER

Gwen Stacy

What are the odds of a second person being bitten by a radioactive spider? Pretty good, as it turns out—because that's exactly what happened to Gwen Stacy! She was bitten while attending a science demonstration about radioactivity.

Before she became a spidery Super Hero, Gwen was a brilliant science student at Midtown High. She loved to spend time in the laboratory working on all kinds of different experiments. A wizard with electronics, Gwen could build cool gadgets that other kids could only dream of. She was going to need those skills to team up with Spidey!

Just like Peter, Gwen can predict danger with her spidey-sense, has the speed and strength of a spider, and can stick to walls. Now Gwen gets to fight crime as Ghost-Spider!

'Come on, guys—keep up!' Ghost-Spider said. She was swinging high above the streets of New York City. Another kid might have been scared out of their wits by the extreme heights. But not Ghost-Spider!

The web-slinging Super Hero was racing against her friends to see who could get to school first. Who were her friends? Glad you asked! Swinging right behind her was Peter Parker, aka Spider-Man, and behind HIM was Miles Morales. Who's Miles Morales? Just turn the page and you'll find out!

'Man, is she fast!' Miles exclaimed.

'There's no way we're going to win this one!' Spider-Man said.

But before Ghost-Spider could respond, her spider-sense went wild. Turn to **page 47** to find out why!

HEIGHT: 170 CM

WEIGHT: 65.8 KG

SUPERHUMAN STRENGTH

SUPERHUMAN AGILITY

SUPERHUMAN ENDURANCE

STICKING TO AND CLIMBING WALLS AND OTHER SURFACES

WEB-SHOOTERS

CAN CAMOUFLAGE HIMSELF AND HIS CLOTHING, BECOMING NEARLY INVISIBLE

DISCHARGES POWERFUL ELECTRICAL VENOM STRIKES

'SPIDER-SENSE' THAT WARNS OF INCOMING DANGER

SPIDER-MAN

Miles Morales

Guess what! Peter Parker and Gwen Stacy aren't the only spiders in town! Meet Miles Morales, a high school student and friend of Peter Parker and Gwen Stacy. Miles was bitten by a—you guessed it—spider! This one was genetically modified instead of radioactive.

With his new-found spider-powers, Miles joined Spider-Man and Ghost-Spider in their fight against crime. Not only does Miles have the speed and strength of a spider and the same spidey-senses that Peter and Gwen have, but he also has a venom strike—a powerful form of energy that he can use to fight off the biggest bad guys in the city. Bonus: Miles can turn invisible, too! These powers come in handy whenever he fights crime in the city—whether it's by himself or as part of the spider-people team.

Have you ever faced the rampaging Rhino? No? Of course you haven't. But it's all in a day's work for Miles Morales!

One day, Miles Morales was on a school excursion to Central Park.

As Peter lay on his back after being charged at by Rhino, Miles rushed over to see if he was okay. 'Hey, Pe—uh, I mean, Spider-Man,' Miles said. Peter was still a little woozy from hitting the ground. 'Miles! Great to see you, buddy . . .' But before Peter could finish, he felt Rhino's hand grab his ankle.

Rhino flung Spidey through the air. As Peter whizzed by, he asked Miles, 'How are your grades holding uuuuup?' Peter was tossed out of sight.

Rhino stormed off to find Peter Parker. But what Rhino didn't realise was that Miles was also a Spider-Man.

Without another thought, Miles slipped on his mask and pulled on his suit.

'Hey, hornhead!' Miles said, swinging above New York City's Central Park. 'Didn't you see the "No Rhinos Allowed" sign?'

'I don't think he's much of a reader,' Spidey said.

'Enough talk!' Rhino said, and he charged the Super Heroes. 'I'm gonna run right over you clowns and flatten you like a couple of, uh, clowns!'

'I'll take the high road!' Miles shouted, and unleashed his venom strike at Rhino.

'And I'll take the low road!' Spidey answered, webbing Rhino's feet.

WHAM!

The Super Villain hit the ground hard.

'You spider-people are the worst,' Rhino said, right before he passed out.

'Do you want to make the final wisecrack?' Peter asked.

Miles smiled. 'How's this? Spider-Men: we put the NO in Rhino.'

Peter burst into laughter and let out a theatrical sob. 'My little baby is all grown up!'

HEIGHT: 160 CM

WEIGHT: 52.2 KG

SUPERHUMAN STRENGTH

SUPERHUMAN AGILITY

SUPERHUMAN ENDURANCE

STICKING TO AND CLIMBING WALLS AND OTHER SURFACES

WEB-SHOOTERS

'SPIDER-SENSE' THAT WARNS OF INCOMING DANGER

SPIDER-GIRL

Anya Corazon

Teenager Anya Corazon was granted amazing spider-like powers after a freak accident. She decided to use her new-found abilities to help protect the city of Brooklyn.

Anya loved swinging around her city. She loved seeing the hustle around Brooklyn and she knew that she was one of the people that could keep it safe.

Sure, the community of arachnid heroes was growing, but Anya has always made sure that she was always there to help protect the weak.

HEIGHT: 178 CM

WEIGHT: 81.6 KG

SUPERHUMAN STRENGTH

SUPERHUMAN AGILITY

SUPERHUMAN ENDURANCE

SHARP TALONS ON HIS HANDS AND FEET THAT CAN BE USED BOTH OFFENSIVELY AND TO CLIMB WALLS

ENHANCED HEARING AND VISION

ORGANIC WEB-SPINNERS IN EACH WRIST THAT ALLOWS HIM TO CREATE AND FIRE HIS OWN WEBBING

SUIT CONTAINS FUTURISTIC FEATURES LIKE INCREASED DURABILITY, HOLOGRAPHIC CAMOUFLAGE AND ADVANCED ARTIFICIAL INTELLIGENCE

SPIDER-MAN 2099

Miguel O'Hara

Coming from an alternate future where the corrupt Alchemax corporation took over New York City, Miguel O'Hara was inspired by the legendary Spider-Man. That was when he decided to put his brain to use and became a similarly powered individual.

Miguel wanted the world to be a better place and he thought that Spider-Man was the answer. Although his efforts weren't quite working out, an attempt to sabotage Miguel's experiments left him on the receiving end of fantastic spider powers! With a futuristic costume equipped with high-tech gear, Miguel is set on undoing the damage done to the world by Alchemax, becoming a new Spider-Man for the year 2099.

VILLAINS

HEIGHT: 180 CM

WEIGHT: 79.3 KG

MASTER OF PHYSICAL STUNT WORK AND MECHANICAL AND VISUAL SPECIAL EFFECTS

SUIT INCLUDES GLASS HELMET WITH THIRTY-MINUTE AIR SUPPLY, HOLOGRAPHIC PROJECTORS, AS WELL AS GLOVES AND BOOTS THAT EMIT HALLUCINOGENIC GAS

SKILLED ACTOR

TRAINED IN HYPNOTISM AND BASIC PSYCHIATRY

CREATED HIS OWN VERSION OF SPIDER-MAN'S WEBBING

MYSTERIO

Quentin Beck

Meet Mysterio, the master of illusion! Except right now, he's the master of getting kicked in the face by the Amazing Spider-Man.

Peter Parker was heading into work at the *Daily Bugle,* when an explosion of green and purple smoke erupted from the top floor of the *Daily Bugle* building!

Switching into his Spider-Man suit, he swung towards the top floor and entered the smoky office.

'The Amazing Spider-Man!' Mysterio began. 'You're right on time . . . to meet your doom!' Mysterio raised his arms and the newsroom filled with thick green smoke.

'Meet my doom?' Spider-Man said. 'What do you suppose he meant by that?'

'Get him, Mysterio!' J. Jonah Jameson yelled. He was the publisher of the *Daily Bugle* newspaper. He really, really didn't like Spider-Man, and had hired Mysterio to defeat the wall-crawler.

It was a trap!

'Oh is that what he meant by doom? Sorry to disappoint you, Mysterio, but I don't have plans to meet my doom for at least another sixty or seventy years!' Spidey said. With unbelievable strength and speed, the Amazing Spider-Man kicked Mysterio in the chest and then fired another web at Jameson, sticking him to the wall.

'I think the only thing Mysterio's going to get is jail time!' Spidey said.

'Curse you, Spider-Man!' Mysterio said as Spider-Man webbed him up. 'How did you see through my illusions?'

'It was easy,' Spidey said. 'I just closed my eyes!'

HEIGHT: 203 CM

WEIGHT: 249.5 KG

SUPERHUMAN STRENGTH

SUPERHUMAN STAMINA

SUPERHUMAN AGILITY

SUPERHUMAN DURABILITY

RESISTANT TO CONVENTIONAL INJURIES

INFLICTS GRAVE INJURIES USING HIS SAVAGE TEETH, CLAWS AND WHIP-LIKE TAIL

CAN TELEPATHICALLY COMMUNICATE WITH AND CONTROL NEARBY REPTILES

MEMBER OF THE SINISTER SIX

LIZARD

Dr Curt Connors

The Lizard is really Dr Curt Connors, a friend of Spidey's. In an attempt to regrow his missing right arm, the scientist turned himself into a giant lizard (which, you know, is kind of a problem)!

'Sssstay ssssstill, Sssssspider-Man!' the Lizard hissed.

'Why, sssssso your ssssssnakes can bite me?' Spider-Man teased.

The Lizard was so angry, he lashed out at Spidey with his tail. The web-slinger jumped up, and the tail missed. Then Spidey leaped right at the Lizard, and poured a vial down the creature's throat! The vial contained an antidote that turned the Lizard back into Dr Connors.

'How can I ever thank you, Spider-Man?' the doctor asked.

'You could get these snakes away from me,' Spidey joked.

HEIGHT: 178 CM

WEIGHT: 77.1 KG

RECEIVED SPOTS AND POWERS BY INADVERTENTLY VISITING THE SPOTTED DIMENSION WHEN ATTEMPTING TO MIMIC PORTALS UTILISED BY THE HERO CLOAK

CAN TELEPORT USING HIS SPOTS, WHICH CAN BE SUSPENDED IN MIDAIR

SCIENTIST SPECIALISING IN PHYSICS

CANNOT THROW AN UNLIMITED NUMBER OF SPACE WARPS AS THEY ARE DRAWN FROM HIS OWN BODY

THE SPOT

Jonathan Ohnn

The Spot is a scientist named Jonathan Ohnn who can summon big black spots. He can walk into one spot and exit from another! He can also stick his hand through a spot to attack Spider-Man!

'How about some PUNCH, Spider-Man?' The Spot laughed.

'No thanks,' Spidey said. 'I had some before I left the house!'

In case you didn't know, Spidey REALLY didn't like The Spot.

Before The Spot could strike again, Spidey spun a web, sticking the villain's arms to his body.

'I can't summon my spots!' The Spot said.

'Too bad I can summon the cops!' Spidey replied.

HEIGHT: 182 CM

WEIGHT: 107 KG

SEEKS TO DEFEAT SPIDER-MAN TO PROVE HE'S THE GREATEST HUNTER IN THE WORLD

UTILISES HAND-TO-HAND COMBAT AND EXPERT KNIFE-FIGHTING

AFTER INGESTING A MYTHICAL POTION, HE WAS GIVEN SUPERHUMAN STRENGTH, SPEED, STAMINA AND DURABILITY

MASTER HUNTER AND TRACKER

KRAVEN THE HUNTER

Sergei Kravinoff

Kraven is the world's most famous hunter, and he came to New York City to capture the most dangerous prey of all—the wondrous wall-crawler! But Spider-Man had other plans. Plans that didn't involve him getting captured by Kraven!

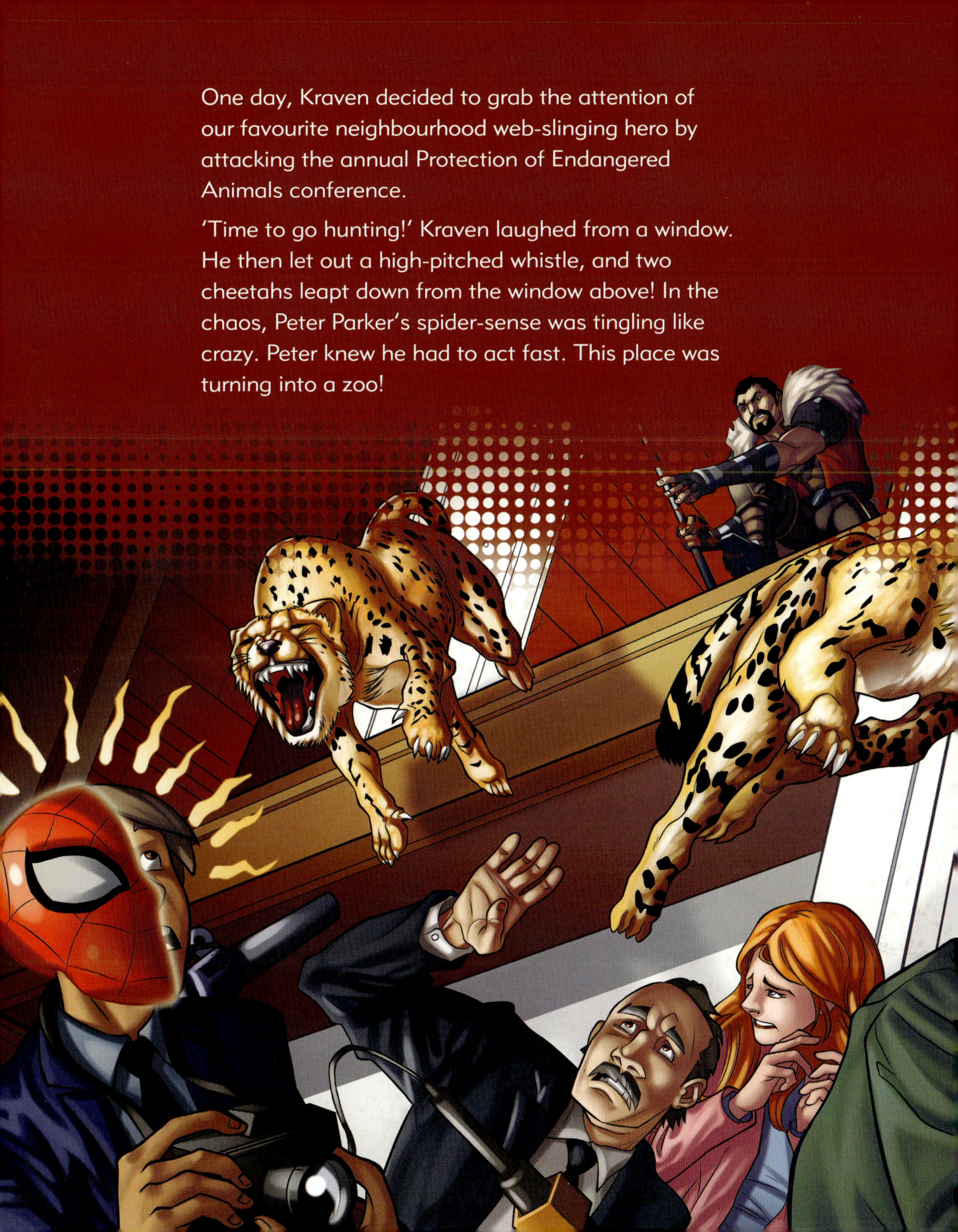

One day, Kraven decided to grab the attention of our favourite neighbourhood web-slinging hero by attacking the annual Protection of Endangered Animals conference.

'Time to go hunting!' Kraven laughed from a window. He then let out a high-pitched whistle, and two cheetahs leapt down from the window above! In the chaos, Peter Parker's spider-sense was tingling like crazy. Peter knew he had to act fast. This place was turning into a zoo!

Once Peter was able to find a place with no-one around, he got into his Spidey suit.

The webbed hero swung into action.

WHOOSH!

'Ah and there is my prey,' Kraven said, smugly.

Kraven's knives sliced through the air, just missing Spider-Man. He began throwing knives at the web-slinging hero. Unfortunately for Kraven, Spidey's trusty spider-sense made it impossible for him to land an attack.

'What's the matter? Can't catch a little Spider?' Spider-Man asked. 'Guess I'll have to catch YOU instead!' Spidey said, spinning his webs, ensnaring the hunter.

The web-slinger had turned the tables!

HEIGHT: 180 CM

WEIGHT: 72.6 KG

INVENTOR WHO CREATED HIS WINGED HARNESS AND USES IT FOR A LIFE OF CRIME

SUPERHUMAN STRENGTH WHEN USING HIS MECHANICAL HARNESS

FLIGHT AT HIGH SPEEDS WITH HARNESS

RAZOR-SHARP TALONS WITH HARNESS, CAPABLE OF TEARING THROUGH STEEL

ADVANCED ENGINEERING SKILLS

VULTURE

Adrian Toomes

The Vulture is really a guy named Adrian Toomes. Toomes created an incredible flying harness that allowed him to take to the skies. Instead of using this new-found power for good, Toomes decided to use it for his own twisted purposes. He's a bad guy is what we're saying.

The Vulture had stolen a fortune in rare diamonds, but Spider-Man wasn't going to let him get away with it!

Man, I sure wish I could fly, Spidey thought. Suddenly the web-slinger heard the sound of rocket engines, and Iron Man soared into view.

'Need a hand, web-head?' Iron Man asked.

'Two against one!' the Vulture sneered. 'That's not fair!'

'Neither is stealing!' Spidey shouted as the heroes grounded the Vulture for good.

HEIGHT: VARIABLE

WEIGHT: VARIABLE

SYMBIOTIC BEING WHO HAS BONDED ITSELF TO A HUMAN HOST

AMORPHOUS COSTUME-LIKE ENTITY WHO CAN TAKE A VARIETY OF SHAPES AND CAMOUFLAGE ITSELF

GRANTS ITS HOST SUPERHUMAN STRENGTH, AGILITY, AND DURABILITY

EXTRUDES TENDRILS AND A LONG TONGUE

CAN CREATE AND PROJECT A WEB-LIKE FLUID FROM ITS OWN SUBSTANCE

CAN MIMIC SPIDER-MAN'S POWERS

MEMBER OF THE SINISTER SIX

VENOM

Eddie Brock

Venom is one weird dude! Part man and part alien creature, Venom really doesn't like Spider-Man and his friends. He even has most of the same powers as Spider-Man. Venom can climb up walls, and he is super-strong. Oh, and let's not forget about the scary teeth!

'Three little spiders!' Venom growled. 'I can't wait to stomp on you!'

Venom screamed and lashed out with his tendrils. They hit Spider-Man hard!

Miles tried to stop him, but the creature just shrugged off the attack.

'Hey, ugly! Over here!' Ghost-Spider yelled, drawing Venom's attention. Then she held out her sound cannon. Ghost-Spider remembered Venom's weakness—really loud sounds. So she cranked up the volume and blasted Venom right in the ear.

'Aaarrrgh!' Venom shouted as the Spiders caught the creature.

HEIGHT:
UNKNOWN

WEIGHT:
UNKNOWN

MASTER OF DISGUISE

INITIALLY DESIGNED A COSTUME THAT COULD MIMIC ANY CLOTHING, INCLUDING A HOLOGRAPHIC BELT THAT COULD STORE THE APPEARANCES OF PEOPLE HE CAME INTO CONTACT WITH TO USE WHENEVER HE NEEDED

EVENTUALLY USED A SERUM THAT ALLOWED HIM TO CHANGE HIS APPEARANCE AT WILL

CHAMELEON

Dmitri Smerdyakov

Chameleon was originally a spy named Dmitri Smerdyakov (try saying that ten times fast!). Not only was Chameleon a spy, he was also a master of disguise. Chameleon realised he could use this to his advantage! Now he can make himself look like anyone else. He can even trick Super Heroes into thinking he is one of the good guys! Which makes him a pretty bad guy.

'Ow!' Spidey yelled. 'Why are you hitting ME?'

'Put Nick Fury down!' Iron Man ordered. He had just arrived on the deck of the helicarrier, only to see Spidey fighting with the leader of S.H.I.E.L.D.

'That's not Fury!' Spidey said. 'That's my old enemy— the Chameleon!'

'He's lying!' Fury replied.

'Oh yeah?' Spidey said, spinning a web at Fury's face. He pulled off a mask, revealing Chameleon underneath! 'Now do you believe me?'

'Sorry I ever doubted you, web-head!' Iron Man replied.

HEIGHT: 183 CM

WEIGHT: 83 KG

SUPERHUMAN STRENGTH, STAMINA, DURABILITY AND AGILITY

GENIUS INTELLECT WITH ADVANCED UNDERSTANDING OF VARIOUS SCIENTIFIC FIELDS, INCLUDING CHEMISTRY, ENGINEERING AND GENETICS

UTILISES A VARIETY OF GOBLIN-THEMED WEAPONRY INCLUDING EXPLOSIVE PUMPKIN BOMBS, A HIGH-SPEED GLIDER EQUIPPED WITH VARIOUS ARMAMENTS, RAZOR-SHARP BATWING THROWING PROJECTILES AND GLOVES CAPABLE OF DISCHARGING POWERFUL ELECTRIC BLASTS

MEMBER OF THE SINISTER SIX

GREEN GOBLIN

Norman Osborn

The head of Oscorp, Norman Osborn was one of the most renowned and powerful businessmen and industrialists in New York City. Like every good (bad) Super Villain story, a lab accident happened.

The incident occured in a lab where Oscorp was testing an experimental serum and it gave Norman superhuman abilities. The accident also left him mentally deranged as a side effect of the transformation. Osborn set about to wreak havoc on the streets of New York City as the costumed criminal known as the Green Goblin.

Despite his recurring maniacal efforts to sow chaos throughout the city, the Goblin is kept at bay by the heroic efforts of his long time arch-nemesis, the Amazing Spider-Man.

But Green Goblin was sick of losing to the Amazing Spider-Man . . . especially when there were two of them! So he formed the Sinister Six with a few other Spidey's greatest nemeses—Rhino, Venom, Sandman, Lizard and Dr Octopus. Now the villains were ready to face the heroes. Find out the results of this battle on **page 55**.

HEIGHT: 185 CM

WEIGHT: 86.2 KG

WHEN BONDED TO A HOST, THE SYMBIOTE GRANTS ITS WEARER MASSIVE SUPERHUMAN STRENGTH, AGILITY AND DURABILITY.

AMORPHOUS FORM ALLOWS THE SYMBIOTE TO TAKE A VARIETY OF SHAPES, EXTRUDE TENDRILS, MIMIC CLOTHING AND OTHERWISE CAMOUFLAGE ITSELF

CAN CREATE AND PROJECT A WEB-LIKE FLUID FROM ITS OWN SUBSTANCE

CARNAGE

Cletus Kasady

Created from the alien being known as Venom, the Carnage symbiote is an amorphous life form that can bond with a host, granting it superhuman powers. In a twist of fate that would spell disaster for innocents around the world, the Carnage symbiote encountered and bonded with Cletus Kasady, an unstable and dangerous criminal.

On the odd occasion, Venom and Carnage work together to defeat the wall-crawling hero. Tonight was one such occasion.

The two symbiotes caused a mess in New York City to lure the Super Hero out. And they did manage to . . . but Spidey wasn't happy.

'Guys, didn't we specifically say attacks only on the weekends? I have homework due tomorrow,' sighed Spider-Man as he quickly webbed the two symbiotes to the top of a building.

HEIGHT: 175 CM

WEIGHT: 93 KG

CAN MENTALLY CONTROL THE FOUR MECHANICAL ARMS FUSED TO HIS TORSO

EACH ARM IS INCREDIBLY DURABLE, CAN EXTEND TO MULTIPLE TIMES ITS LENGTH AND IS CAPABLE OF LIFTING SEVERAL TONNES

THE REACTION TIME AND AGILITY OF THESE TENTACLES IS SUPERHUMANLY FAST AND PRECISE

RENOWNED GENIUS IN MULTIPLE SCIENTIFIC FIELDS, INCLUDING PHYSICS, INVENTION, ENGINEERING AND RADIATION.

MEMBER OF THE SINISTER SIX

DOCTOR OCTOPUS

Otto Gunther Octavius

Otto Octavius was a brilliant physicist and inventor. He was well-respected around the science community! But an accident in his laboratory changed everything . . . his greatest invention fused with his body! The same accident left him mentally unstable and now, he wanted to prove that he has the greatest criminal mind!

The team of villains who called themselves the Sinister Six staged an attack against the web-slingers . . . and the villains had the upper hand! But Doc Ock knew that the spiders were smart . . . the Sinister Six needed a plan. But when your team had three geniuses, two strongmen and one symbiote, there wasn't much room for planning and discussion.

Needless to say, the spiders showed better teamwork and defeated the Sinister Six, keeping New York City safe once more.

HEIGHT: 196 CM

WEIGHT: 322.1 KG

MASSIVE SUPERHUMAN STRENGTH AND STAMINA

POSSESSES A THICK, RHINO-HIDE-LIKE POLYMER SUIT COVERING HIS ENTIRE BODY

RHINO-HIDE PROVIDES EXTREME DURABILITY

THE HEAD OF THE SUIT IS OUTFITTED WITH HORNS CAPABLE OF PUNCTURING SOLID STEEL

NOT THE BRIGHTEST VILLAIN AROUND THE BLOCK . . .

MEMBER OF THE SINISTER SIX

RHINO

Aleksei Sytsevich

Originally a low-level and dim-witted thug looking for an easy payout, Aleksei Sytsevich allowed himself to be the subject of a Mafia-run black market experiment. He emerged from the gruelling trial endowed with incredible strength, and bonded to a rhinoceros-like skin of nearly indestructible armour. With his new powers and little else to his name, the Rhino continued his life of crime, selling his brute muscle to any thug or mob boss willing to pay his price.

Miles Morales and his friend Ganke were on an excursion when suddenly . . .

'Ganke, watch out!' Miles shouted to his best friend.

A flood of wild animals came stampeding towards them right in the heart of the Central Park Zoo! 'How did all these animals escape?' Ganke asked.

And the universe answered his question as the Rhino charged out of the woods and came barrelling towards Miles and Ganke.

Well, we know what happened from that point on, just go back to **page 22**!

As you can see, it's not all fun and games being a Spider-Hero. But it's STILL pretty awesome.

'Hey, guys,' Miles said. 'I think Venom just woke up from his nap . . .'

Looks like it's time for our heroes to get back to work!

GUARDIANS OF THE GALAXY

HEIGHT: 185 CM

WEIGHT: 79.4 KG

HALF HUMAN,
HALF ALIEN

ADEPT HAND-TO-HAND COMBATANT AND MARKSMAN

GIFTED STRATEGIST, WITH APTITUDE FOR THINKING OUTSIDE THE BOX

HAS A UNIQUE PAIR OF BLASTERS THAT ONLY WORKS IN HIS HANDS

HIGH-TECH MASK GRANTS A VARIETY OF VISION MODES AND SUPPLIES OXYGEN EVEN IN THE VACUUM OF SPACE

STAR-LORD

Peter Quill

Have you ever been to outer space? Lived in it? Worked in it? Joined forces with four aliens to save the galaxy? No? Same here. But Peter Quill has! As a member of the heroic Guardians of the Galaxy, Peter travels throughout space to right intergalactic wrongs.

It wasn't always that way, though. When he was a kid growing up on Earth, Peter only dreamed of having adventures in outer space. Peter studied and practised very hard to become an astronaut so he could live out those adventures for real!

As Peter grew up, he decided to travel the galaxy and go on great adventures! One of his great wishes was to meet his dad, but it was hard to find him. That was when he realised if he could make a name for himself, his dad might notice him! So, Peter decided that he would be known throughout the galaxy as the great space adventurer, Star-Lord!

During his travels, Star-Lord met many different beings from different planets. But he made some really good friends in Gamora, Drax, Rocket and Groot. They decided to stay together to help anyone in danger anywhere in the cosmos. That was when the Guardians of the Galaxy were born.

And as Star-Lord adventured with his new crew, he realised that they were more important than finding his dad. Because now, the Guardians were his family.

The Guardians had just arrived at their latest mission. Their ship, the *Milano*, hovered in the sky. If anything went wrong on the mission, they would have to make it back to the ship as fast as they could to escape.

'Watch where you're pointin' that thing!' Rocket said as Peter jumped past him. 'I don't wanna get hurt BEFORE we go into battle!'

'Then maybe you should stay behind me,' Peter said. 'I mean, I AM the leader.'

'Will you two stop bickering?' Gamora sighed.

'Yes, this argument is ridiculous,' Drax added, before letting loose a bloodcurdling battle cry.

'I am Groot,' Groot said.

'Fine,' Peter said. 'But stay out of my way, raccoon.'

'I ain't no raccoon!' Rocket said. Peter was pretty sure that he was.

It was just another typical day for the Guardians of the Galaxy.

HEIGHT: 175 CM

WEIGHT: 77.1 KG

ADOPTED DAUGHTER OF THANOS, RAISED WITH HER ADOPTED SISTER, NEBULA

STRENGTH, AGILITY, PHYSICAL CONDITIONING AND HEALING RATE HEIGHTENED BY CYBERNETIC IMPLANTS AND GENETIC ALTERATION

UNPARALLELED WARRIOR, MASTER OF HAND-TO-HAND COMBAT

EXPERIENCE IN VIRTUALLY ALL KNOWN MARTIAL ARTS

PROFICIENT IN A WIDE VARIETY OF WEAPONRY

HIGHLY SKILLED IN THE ART OF SUBTERFUGE

GAMORA

The Deadliest Woman in the Galaxy

If there's anyone more dangerous in the galaxy than Gamora, we haven't met them (we haven't met a lot of people, but that's beside the point)! When Gamora was just a little girl, the Mad Titan, Thanos, came to her planet and wiped out her people, but 'saved' Gamora and trained her to fight better than anyone so he could use her to fight his battles.

Being the most feared Super Villain in the universe, Thanos wanted more powerful warriors that would serve him. So he also adopted another girl, named Nebula (more on her later!), and she became Gamora's sister. But they were forced by Thanos to fight one another constantly. They both became powerful warriors, but because they were always competing, the sisters came to dislike each other.

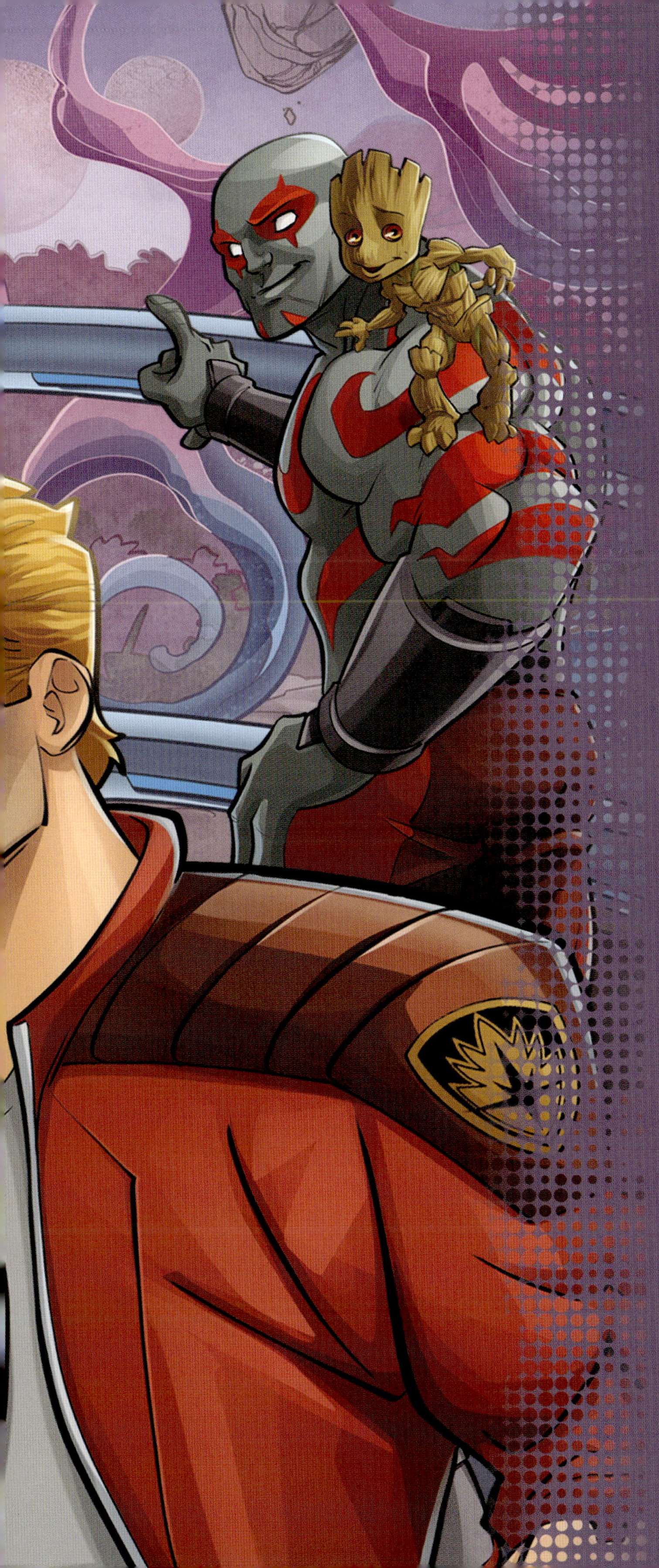

While Nebula grew accustomed to violence, Gamora wanted to help others. She ran away from her evil family in search of something better.

One day, Gamora met Star-Lord. He heard she was a great warrior and wanted to get to know her. Star-Lord tracked down Gamora, and the two bonded instantly. They both didn't want to feel so alone.

Eventually Gamora went against her father and joined the Guardians of the Galaxy. She was an extremely skilled fighter and became known as the deadliest woman in the galaxy (like we mentioned on **page 68**)!

Now, Gamora travels alongside Star-Lord, Drax, Rocket and Groot to try and help any being that is in trouble around the cosmos.

The Guardians had landed on the planet Morag, and it was chaos on the planet's surface. The Guardians had been forced to split up, and Star-Lord was trying to keep track of his team.

'Where are you, Gamora?' Peter said over his comms link. 'I've been trying to reach you for an hour, and all I'm getting is static!'

'I'm running through the streets of an alien city, chasing after my sister!' Gamora said angrily. 'Now stop bothering me!'

'Sheesh,' Peter replied. 'I was just asking a question.'

Gamora had been searching for Nebula, trying to persuade her to join the Guardians.

Suddenly, a bright flash of light appeared, and Gamora couldn't see. When her vision cleared, she saw Thanos sitting on his throne. Nebula was there, too.

'Hello, daughter,' Thanos said. 'Let the combat begin!'

HEIGHT: 196 CM

WEIGHT: 308.4 KG; UP TO 476.2 KG IN MOST POWERFUL BODY

FUELLED BY REVENGE FOR HIS FAMILY

SUPERHUMAN STRENGTH AND DURABILITY

FEROCIOUS HAND-TO-HAND COMBATANT

HIGHLY SKILLED WITH BLADES AND OTHER CLOSE-COMBAT GEAR

DIRECT BUT ROUGH-EDGED IN COMMUNICATION

DRAX

The Destroyer

Gamora wasn't the only incredible warrior who joined the Guardians. A large alien named Drax the Destroyer, who has super-strength, also joined Peter Quill's space-faring team. Fierce and powerful, Drax is great to have in any battle.

Years ago, Drax lost his family. Since then, he has roamed the galaxy looking for Thanos, who took his family from him. He joined Gamora and Peter, glad to be part of a family once more. Drax is an incredible warrior, braver than anyone the Guardians have ever met. But Drax has one teeny, tiny flaw. He takes everything literally. For example, if you said something was so funny you forgot to laugh, from then on Drax would remind you to laugh. You know, so you wouldn't forget!

'Something's wrong with Iron Man!' Star-Lord said.

'That is obvious,' Drax replied. Remember when we said that he took everything very literally? Well, he was doing it again. 'He is acting like a jerk.'

'I don't think he's acting,' Rocket added.

'Drax!' Star-Lord shouted. 'Get the people out of here before Shellhead does some serious damage!'

As Iron Man blasted the Guardians of the Galaxy, Drax moved quickly. He protected one of his friends, the mechanic that was helping fix the *Milano*. Drax was loyal to those who most needed help.

Suddenly, a voice rang out overhead. 'Need a hand?'

The Guardians looked up to see Thor, the Mighty Avenger!

'What's Thunderhead doing here?' Rocket said, looking up at Thor.

'I was on a mission to Xandar and heard the same distress signal you did,' Thor replied.

Thor joined the Guardians in the battle but Iron Man was still attacking!

Suddenly, a green blur jumped out from a building behind Iron Man and slammed into the rampaging Avenger, knocking him to the ground.

'Hulk smash!'

Now with Iron Man down, everyone wanted to know what happened to their friend.

Star-Lord bent down to open Iron Man's helmet to find there was no-one inside. 'The suit is empty. But . . . it looks like his arc reactor has been tampered with!'

'Let me see it,' Rocket said, examining the blinking gadget. 'Hmm . . . I've seen these before. It's an ordinary tracking device. You can get them anywhere.'

Everyone gave a sigh of relief. It was good to know that their friend wasn't evil.

HEIGHT: 91 CM

WEIGHT: UNKNOWN

NOT A RACCOON

MASTER PILOT, ENGINEER, MARKSMAN AND WEAPONS SPECIALIST

GENETICALLY AND CYBERNETICALLY ENHANCED

HIGHLY AGILE

MECHANICAL GENIUS (ESPECIALLY IN ENGINEERING, VEHICLES AND HEAVY MUNITIONS)

TOUGH TALKER

ROCKET

Not a Raccoon

If you travel the galaxy far and wide, you'll never meet anyone like Rocket! That's because only Rocket is like Rocket! That makes sense, right? Anyway, Rocket was kind of like a raccoon, we guess, until a team of scientists experimented upon the little guy. He has all the abilities of a raccoon—a heightened sense of sight, sound and smell—but he was also given increased intelligence. That Rocket is one smart creature!

Even though he may look like a furry, fuzzy woodland creature, Rocket is anything but. He's tough, scrappy and always ready for a fight. And if you call him a 'raccoon', you'll find all that out really quick (hint: don't call him a raccoon)! Rocket's also a master of all kinds of weapons, and comes up with great battle plans. Rocket's best friend is a talking tree named Groot. Together, they joined the Guardians of the Galaxy and when they're not fighting with each other, they're saving the universe. Or parts of it, anyway.

The Guardians landed on a planet called Blorf, for a mission. Star-Lord, Gamora and Drax went to deliver the package while Rocket and Groot were put in charge of cleaning the *Milano*.

Rocket wanted to see if the old cleaning bot would work . . . it didn't. Instead, it ran off the ship and went outside.

The bot attracted the attention of a group of pig-like aliens called Kodabaks. The Kodabaks didn't like the commotion so they decided to attack it!

Rocket wasn't sure what to do. But luckily Groot had a suggestion. 'I am Groot!' he exclaimed.

'That's a great idea! Thanks, buddy!' said Rocket. He grabbed his size-changing ray and aimed it at the Kodabaks.

'You feeling lucky, pigs? I know I am.'

SHAZACK!

Rocket blasted the beasts with purple energy, shrinking them down.

'This is my chance to save the day! I've got to act fast,' Rocket said. With tool in hand, he jumped onto the bot's back. In an instant, it was fixed. 'Watch this!'

The cleaning bot swept the tiny Kodabaks up into its dustpan without a second thought. Then, the bot raced into the *Milano* as quick as lightning.

'Look at it go!' Rocket shouted. And in no time, the *Milano* was spotless.

When Star-Lord, Gamora and Drax returned from their mission, they were impressed by how clean everything looked.

'Nice work, Rocket,' Star-Lord said. 'The *Milano* looks great.'

Rocket grinned. 'I can't take all the credit,' he said, picking up Groot. 'After all, I did have a little help.'

HEIGHT:
VARIABLE

WEIGHT:
VARIABLE

MEMBER OF A TREE-LIKE ALIEN RACE

SUPERHUMAN STRENGTH

ABILITY TO REGENERATE AFTER ENDURING PHYSICAL DAMAGE

PLANT-LIKE FORM ENABLES HIM TO GROW OR RESHAPE HIS LIMBS AND ROOT HIMSELF IN PLACE FOR ENHANCED STABILITY

CAN EMIT GLOWING SPORES

ONLY SAYS THE PHRASE 'I AM GROOT'

GROOT

He is Groot

This is Groot! He's a tree. Well, sort of. He comes from Planet X, where a race of tree-like beings dwell. The only thing Groot can say is 'I am Groot'. At least, that's what it sounds like to us. But to somebody who speaks Groot's language, it can mean practically anything!

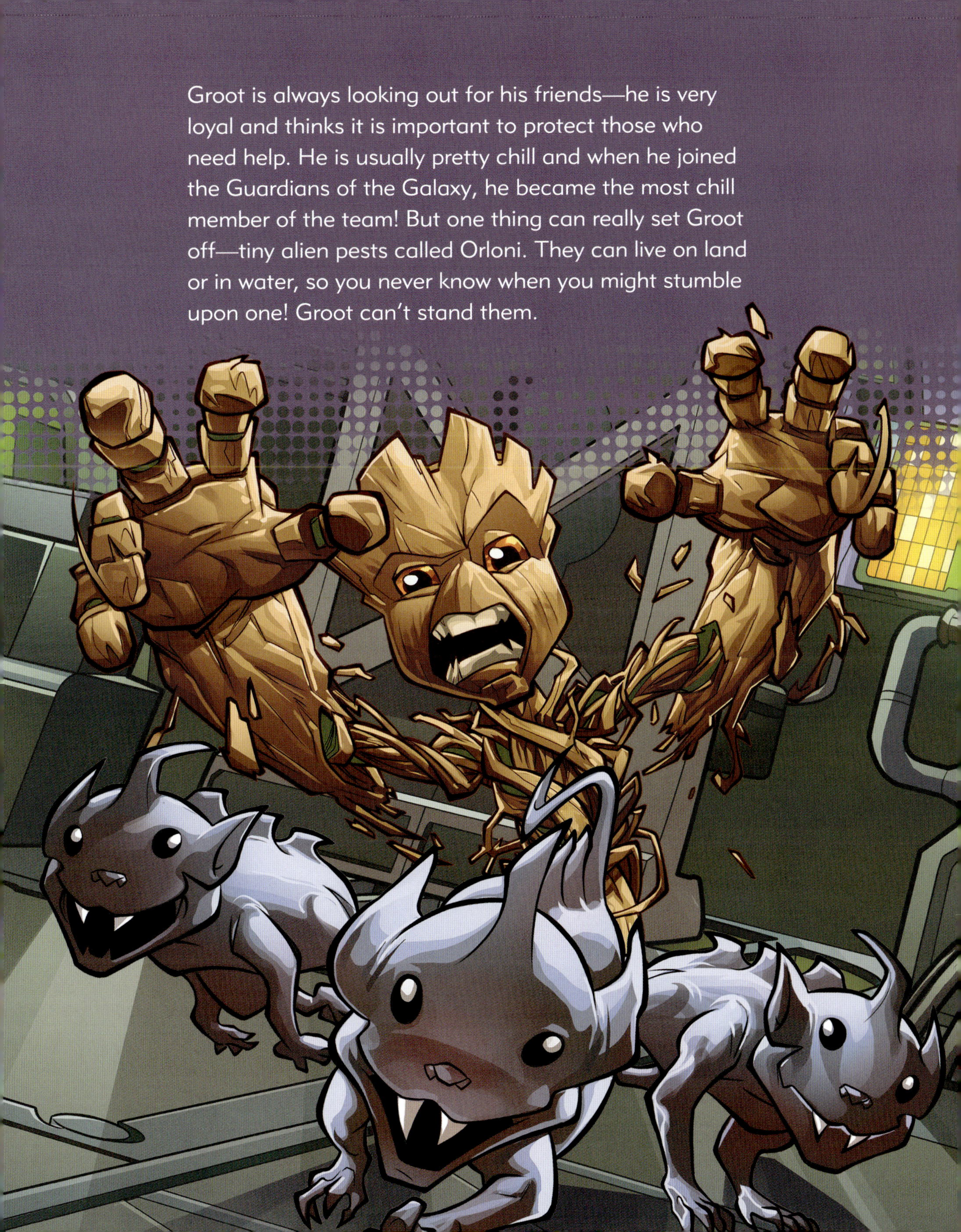

Groot is always looking out for his friends—he is very loyal and thinks it is important to protect those who need help. He is usually pretty chill and when he joined the Guardians of the Galaxy, he became the most chill member of the team! But one thing can really set Groot off—tiny alien pests called Orloni. They can live on land or in water, so you never know when you might stumble upon one! Groot can't stand them.

'I AM GROOT!' he shouted.

Something was wrong with the Guardians' ship, the *Milano*. The engines wouldn't work! Groot suspected that the pesky Orloni were responsible.

'*RAWWWR!*' With a fierce scream, Groot jumped towards the pests. But the Orloni scattered away just in time. Groot didn't hesitate and chased after the creatures. No Orloni was going to cause mischief while he was around!

Groot was able to find two of the Orloni pretty quickly. He was fast and small which made him the perfect Guardian to find the Orloni. But where was that last one?

Groot got his friend Rocket to help him find the last one. They were at the main pipe when Groot got an idea. 'I am Groot?'

But Rocket wasn't so sure. 'I guess you're small enough to fit, but it's way too dangerous. One wrong move and you could blow up the whole ship.'

Suddenly, Groot saw something run past. The last Orloni! Groot ran after the Orloni as it scampered into the main pipe.

'*GRRAWWWR!*' shouted Groot as he chased the last pesky Orloni down the main pipe. He knew that was what he shouldn't have done . . . but it was the only way to see what was wrong!

'Get outta there, Groot!' Rocket yelled. He was worried for his friend!

'I am Groot!' Groot replied as he kept after the Orloni. He was determined to catch the alien wreaking havoc on his ship!

Soon, the Orloni raced right into a big blob of engine goo (yes, that's a thing). The Orloni was using it to build a nest! The Orloni was afraid of Groot and burst right through the blob. Now the engines would work!

'Great job, pal!' Rocket said. 'But next time, try not to jump into the engine, okay?'

'I am Groot!'

MILANO

Home of the Guardians

Peter Quill's trusty starship acts as the primary mode of transportation for the Guardians of the Galaxy. A one-of-a-kind vehicle for a one-of-a-kind team, the *Milano* can outrun, outmanoeuvre and outclass anyone foolish enough to give the Guardians chase.

HEIGHT: BIG!!!

WEIGHT: HEAVY!!!

M-SHIP USED BY RAVAGERS

IMPRESSIVE ARSENAL OF INTERSTELLAR WEAPONS

INTERSTELLAR FLIGHTS

VERY FAST SHIP TO EVADE ANY BIG ATTACKS FROM ENEMIES

COOLEST GADGETS TO MAKE THE SHIP A HOME FOR THE GUARDIANS

The *Milano* was first given to Star-Lord before he even became Star-Lord. Back when he still went by Peter Quill, the Ravagers (you're going to meet their leader on **page 98**!) gave him the ship. These types of ships were made for scouting and hunting purposes.

Star-Lord loved flying the *Milano* but even with all the flying, before Star-Lord met the rest of the Guardians, the ship just felt like a vehicle. Now, it felt like home.

'Star-Lord, on your left!' Iron Man shouted over the battle. Kree soldiers, warriors from a vengeful alien race, had launched an attack on the planet Xandar.

The fighting was fierce and soon, Xandar had fallen into total chaos. Outnumbered, the Guardians and the Avengers tried to escape and regroup, but something was wrong. The *Milano* wouldn't start!

'Rocket, Groot, fix the ship. We need to leave pronto!' shouted Star-Lord while defending against the Kree.

While the battle raged on, Groot was able to find the source of the problem . . . pesky Orlonis (read more about them from **page 87**)!

Now that the Orloni problem was fixed, Rocket called out to the other heroes. 'Okay, we're set, now let's get outta here!'

In the cockpit, Star-Lord set the thrusters to full power, and the *Milano* took off with a jolt, dodging fire from the Kree army as it ascended into space.

The *Milano* kept not only the Guardians but the Avengers safe once again!

HEIGHT: 168 CM

WEIGHT: 52.2 KG

TELEPATHY

EMPATHY, TO SENSE OTHERS' EMOTIONS

SELF-HEALING

PRECOGNITION TO FORESEE EVENTS BEFORE THEY UNFOLD

TO TRAVEL IN SPACE, MANTIS PROJECTS HER ASTRAL FORM FROM HER BODY, ALLOWING HER TO TRAVEL INTERPLANETARY DISTANCES

PHYSICALLY ENHANCED DURABILITY AS WELL AS IMMUNITY TO MENTAL AND METAPHYSICAL ASSAULTS

MANTIS

Chick with the Antennae

An unusual alien being who travels the cosmos seeking truth, Mantis has encountered the Guardians of the Galaxy on numerous occasions. Though her motives are not always clear, she has proven herself a reliable and compassionate ally.

Mantis had a pretty lonely childhood, so when she first met the Guardians, she was a little aloof. But after being able to connect with equally-aloof Drax, she soon felt at home with the Guardians and was excited to be able to fight alongside her new family in protecting innocent beings all over the cosmos.

HEIGHT: 188 CM / 216 CM WITH CYBERNETIC FIN

WEIGHT: 92.3 KG

ACCOMPLISHED TACTICIAN AND STRATEGIST

NUMEROUS UNDERWORLD CONNECTIONS

COMMANDS THE VAST FLEET OF RAVAGERS AND EMPLOYS A VARIETY OF ADVANCED VEHICLES AND WEAPONS, OFTEN STOLEN FROM OTHER SHIPS

HAS A TECHNOLOGICALLY ADVANCED FLYING ARROW CONTROLLED BY A FIN IMPLANTED IN HIS HEAD

BY WHISTLING IN DIFFERENT PITCHES AND CADENCES, HE CAN PRECISELY CONTROL THE ARROW'S VELOCITY AND DIRECTION

YONDU UDONTA

Leader of the Ravagers

Yondu Udonta acts as leader of the Ravagers, a ruthless army of unscrupulous space pirates and mercenaries. Long ago, he was hired to capture the young Earthling Peter Quill, aka Star-Lord, though a last-minute change of heart caused Yondu to betray his employer and bring Quill into the fold as one of his own, serving almost as a surrogate father.

As the leader of the Ravagers, Yondu leads the charge in most of their missions. He sometimes would send Star-Lord to help the team. Yondu does have a soft spot for the human but sometimes . . . Yondu's greed causes him to betray even his closest allies any time the promise of some quick credits is involved.

VILLAINS

HEIGHT: 196 CM

WEIGHT: UNKNOWN

SUPREME ACCUSER OF THE KREE EMPIRE, DEDICATED TO JUSTICE AND ANCIENT TRADITION

SUPERHUMAN STRENGTH, ENDURANCE, AGILITY AND DURABILITY

EXPERT HAND-TO-HAND COMBATANT, WITH MASTERY OVER A VARIETY OF KREE FIGHTING STYLES

WIELDS THE UNIVERSAL WEAPON, A HAMMER-LIKE STAFF CAPABLE OF ABSORBING AND PROJECTING ENERGY, MANIPULATING GRAVITATIONAL FORCES AND INFLICTING MASSIVE PHYSICAL DEVASTATION

EXPERIENCED SOLDIER WITH A HONED MILITARY MIND

RONAN

The Accuser

As you might have guessed, the galaxy is full of bad guys—bad guys like Ronan the Accuser. Ronan is a Kree warrior who wants to punish anyone who stands in his way. And unfortunately for the Guardians, they're usually standing in his way!

Ronan had found Drax, who was trying to protect a group of aliens from the Kree's wrath. Ronan was wielding the cosmi-rod, a weapon that gave Ronan great power.

'You are a monster,' Drax said. 'And you'll harm no-one. I won't allow it!'

'You are in a position to allow nothing,' Ronan said, unleashing a blast at Drax.

But Ronan had not counted on Drax's incredible strength, or his ability to withstand pain. 'If that's the best you can do,' Drax said, 'you might want to run.'

Ronan was starting to think that Drax was right!

HEIGHT: 187 CM

WEIGHT: 204.1 KG

INTERGALACTIC DEALER AND COLLECTOR OF RARE AND UNUSUAL ITEMS

INFAMOUS FOR HIS ECCENTRIC TASTES

CONTROLS AN EXPANSIVE ESTATE

HAS NUMEROUS POLITICAL AND CRIMINAL CONNECTIONS ACROSS THE GALAXY

POSSESSES GREAT WEALTH AND RESOURCES

SEEKS TO PURCHASE OR ACQUIRE TECHNOLOGY, WEAPONS, SERVICES AND MORE AS PART OF HIS VAST COLLECTION

THE COLLECTOR

Taneleer Tivan

While some might not call The Collector a villain, he certainly has a wicked side. One of the Elders of the Universe, The Collector spends his days acquiring anything and everything that catches his interest. Usually it's rare, one-of-a-kind objects that attract his attention—and in some cases it isn't objects, but rare, one-of-a-kind beings!

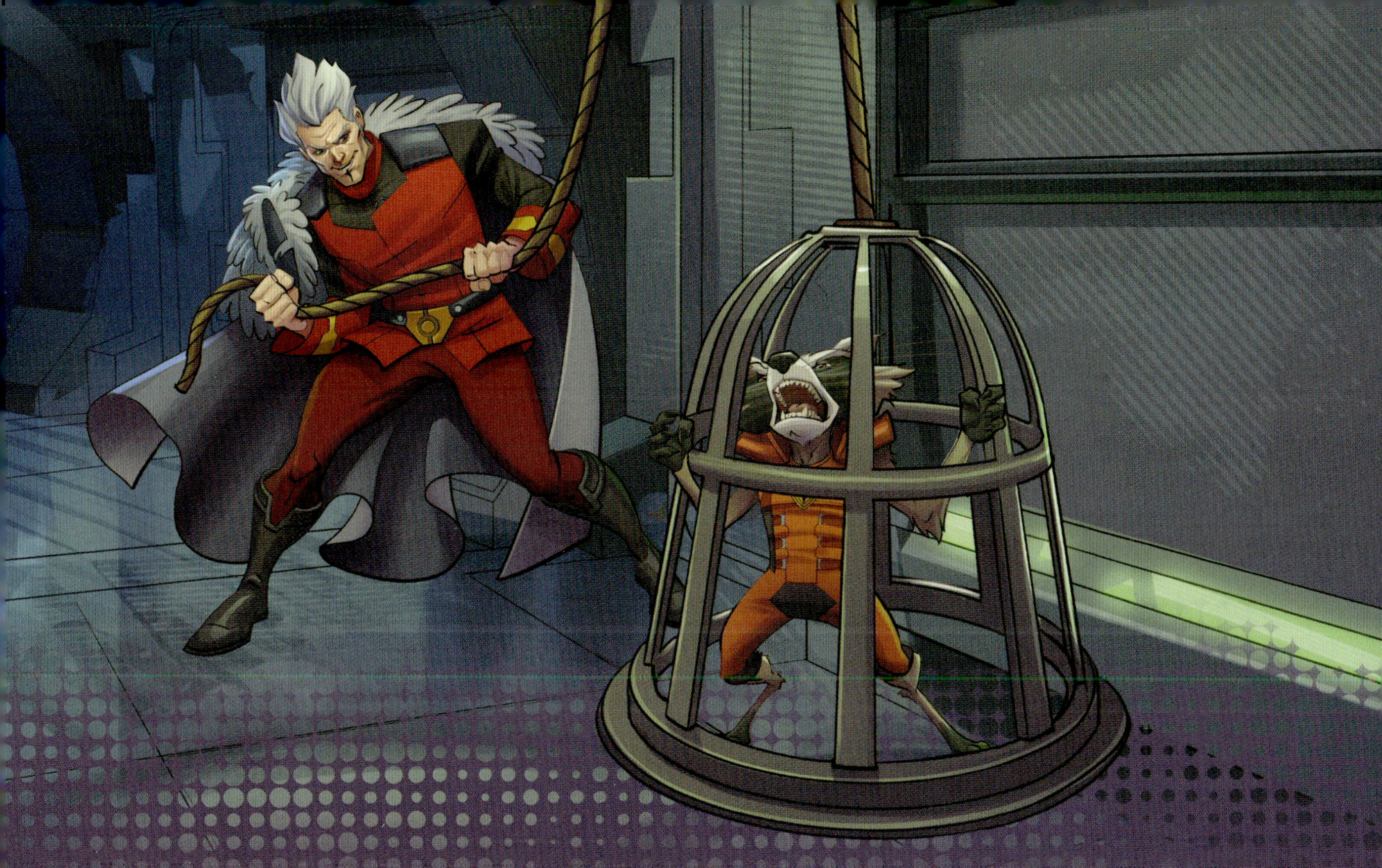

Perhaps that's why The Collector had his sights set on Rocket!

'What manner of creature are you?' The Collector said.

'I ain't no creature,' the tiny Guardian snarled. 'I'm Rocket!'

'Regardless,' The Collector said, 'I will add you to my collection.' He pressed a button on a control pad, springing an elaborate trap. But Rocket pried the bars open. He jumped atop the villain's head and pulled his hair.

'Ahhh!' The Collector shouted. 'What are you doing?!'

'Say you'll leave me alone, and I'll stop,' Rocket replied.

'Fine!' The Collector said. 'You seem more annoying than you're worth anyway. Begone.'

HEIGHT: 180 CM

WEIGHT: 83.9 KG

MERCILESS SPACE PIRATE

ADOPTED DAUGHTER OF THANOS AND ADOPTED SISTER OF GAMORA

HEIGHTENED STRENGTH, AGILITY, DURABILITY AND REFLEXES DUE TO EXTENSIVE CYBERNETIC AUGMENTATION

SKILLED PHYSICAL COMBATANT, WITH EXPERTISE IN A VARIETY OF ADVANCED WEAPONRY

CUNNING TACTICIAN, MANIPULATOR AND STRATEGIST

SEEKS TO ACHIEVE VICTORY AND POWER BY ANY MEANS

NEBULA

Daughter of Thanos

Do you remember back on **page 69** when we said we'd tell you more about Nebula later? Well, now it's later! Nebula is a cunning warrior and every bit as deadly as her sister, Gamora. Part machine, Nebula's strength and speed have been increased, making her a real threat to the Guardians of the Galaxy. She would destroy them just to get at her sister.

'Ah, Gamora,' Nebula said, 'what a very unpleasant surprise!'

Gamora rolled her eyes. 'Time's up, sister of mine,' she snarled as she lunged at Nebula. But Nebula pressed a button on a device and Gamora froze.

In horror, Gamora watched her arm lower itself and drop her sword. Gamora was powerless to respond. Nebula seemed to be controlling her body with the device!

'Clever, isn't it?' Nebula said. 'They're doing all sorts of wonderful things with technology at Nova Corps these days. Imagine all the trouble I can cause now!'

Just when Nebula thought she had the upper hand, Star-Lord burst into the room. 'Not so fast! When you mess with Gamora, you mess with all of us!'

In the blink of an eye, the Guardians attacked Nebula and was able to free Gamora from being frozen by destroying the device.

Gamora picked up her sword and turned to face Nebula. Now that she was able to move, Gamora overpowered Nebula very quickly.

The Guardians watched as Gamora handcuffed Nebula. 'Now you're the one who can't move, sister,' she said smugly.

Gamora hoped that maybe one day, instead of fighting against each other, she and Nebula could fight together. Then, with their combined might, they could beat Thanos once and for all . . . but today was not that day.

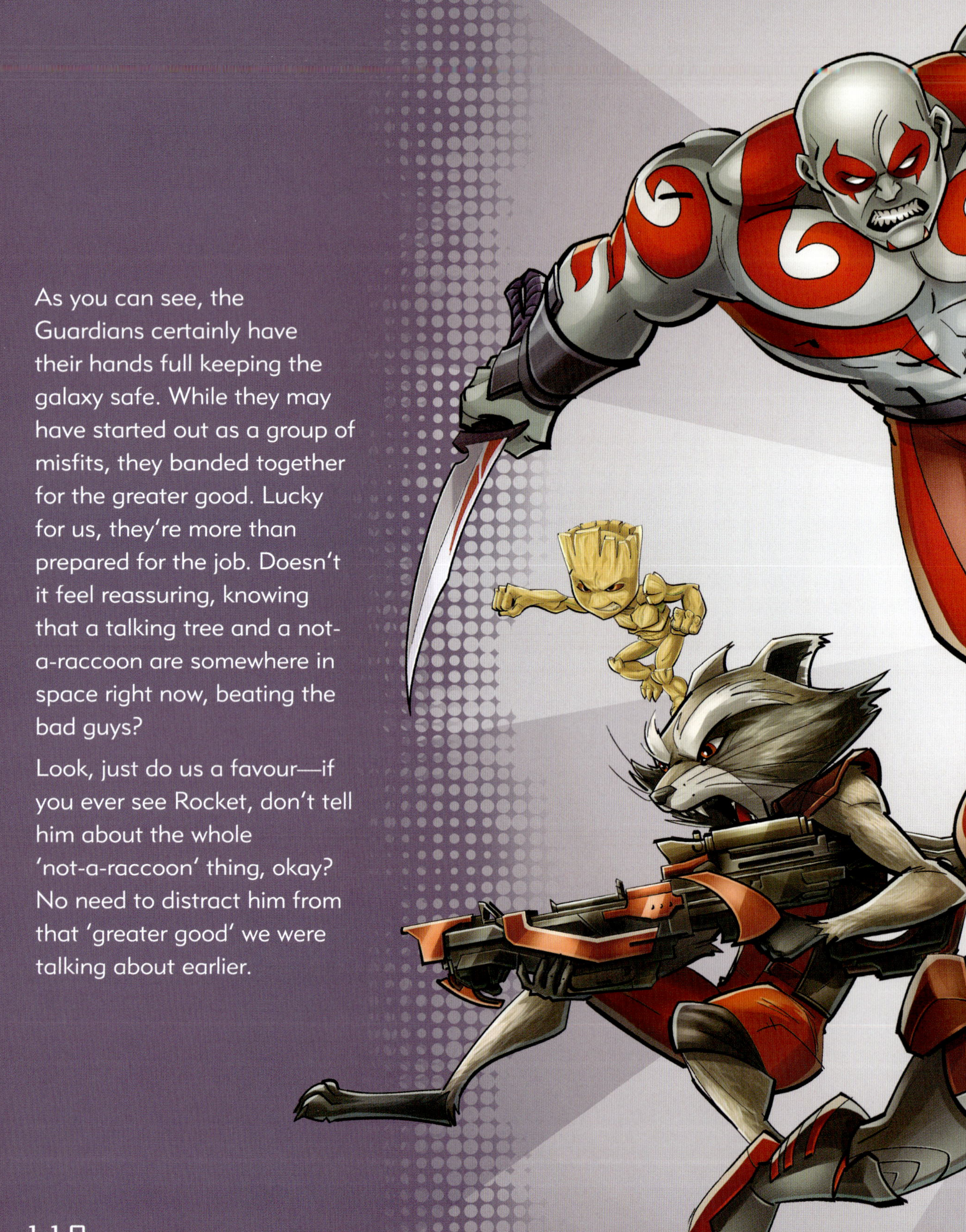

As you can see, the Guardians certainly have their hands full keeping the galaxy safe. While they may have started out as a group of misfits, they banded together for the greater good. Lucky for us, they're more than prepared for the job. Doesn't it feel reassuring, knowing that a talking tree and a not-a-raccoon are somewhere in space right now, beating the bad guys?

Look, just do us a favour—if you ever see Rocket, don't tell him about the whole 'not-a-raccoon' thing, okay? No need to distract him from that 'greater good' we were talking about earlier.

THE AVENGERS

HEIGHT: 185 CM / 196 CM IN ARMOUR

WEIGHT: 86.1 KG / 192.8 KG IN ARMOUR

GENIUS-LEVEL INTELLECT WITH PARTICULAR APTITUDE IN INVENTION AND ENGINEERING

BILLIONAIRE INDUSTRIALIST

WEARS MODULAR ARC-REACTOR-POWERED IRON MAN ARMOUR GRANTING SUPERHUMAN STRENGTH AND DURABILITY

ARMOURED SUIT GRANTS ABILITY TO FLY AND PROJECT REPULSOR BLASTS

ARMOUR IS OUTFITTED WITH COMPLEX TECH, INCLUDING A CUTTING-EDGE ARTIFICIAL INTELLIGENCE, SOPHISTICATED SENSOR SYSTEMS AND OTHER GADGETRY

IRON MAN

Tony Stark

Tony Stark was very rich and incredibly smart. He graduated from college at a very young age and inherited his dad's company, Stark Industries. It made all kinds of weapons and sold them to the army. Tony didn't like to think about how those weapons were used.

But one day, he had no choice. While he was showing some soldiers how to use his weapons, Tony was attacked and held captive by enemies of the United States who wanted Tony to make a weapon for them!

With the help of another prisoner, Dr Ho Yinsen, Tony DID build a weapon. But not the weapon that the bad guys wanted! Instead, Tony built an incredible suit of armour that he used to escape.

Tony felt ashamed that his work was being used by warlords. But along with his shame, Tony also felt something new. There was just a spark of it—a hint of pride that, at least in this one instance, he had taken weapons away from bad men.

Once he got home, Tony decided to stop selling weapons. Instead, he kept working in secret to refine and re-design his Iron Man armour so he could protect the world from the weapons he wouldn't be able to stop.

Tony continuously upgraded his armour and fought tirelessly to keep the world safe. Eventually, he became a founding member of the Mighty Avengers!

Tony Stark wouldn't be remembered for his time creating weapons. Instead, the world came to know him for his red and gold armour. The world soon called him a Super Hero—the Iron Man!

One of the great things about being Iron Man was having a high-tech headquarters in New York City.

One of the not-so-great things about being Iron Man? Evil aliens called Chitauri that attacked his high-tech headquarters in New York City!

'I'm sorry,' Iron Man said as he blasted a Chitauri warrior. 'What part of "stay down" don't you understand?'

As Iron Man kept the enemy busy, the Avengers arrived at the scene, along with the Nova Corps. The Chitauri warriors thought they would conquer Earth easily, but they hadn't counted on Iron Man!

With the help of the other Avengers, Iron Man made short work of the Chitauri and their cybernetic creatures.

'Hulk smash!' Hulk said as he slammed his fists into a metal beast.

'You do good work, Hulk!' Iron Man said.

Captain America smiled as the Avengers saved the day.

HEIGHT: 188 CM

WEIGHT: 104.3 KG

RECIPIENT OF THE SUPER-SOLDIER SERUM

THE PINNACLE OF HUMAN PHYSICAL POTENTIAL

HEIGHTENED STRENGTH, ENDURANCE AND AGILITY

MASTER HAND-TO-HAND FIGHTER

SKILLED MILITARY LEADER AND STRATEGIST WITH A STRONG SENSE OF HONOUR AND JUSTICE

EQUIPPED WITH A VIRTUALLY INDESTRUCTIBLE VIBRANIUM SHIELD

CAPTAIN AMERICA

Steve Rogers

Are you ready to travel back in time? Good! Because we're headed back to the 1940s, when the world was at war! This is where we meet Captain America, but before he was Captain America, he was Steve Rogers!

Frail Steve Rogers wanted to serve his country, but the U.S. Army told him that he was too small and not healthy enough. But a man named Dr Erskine thought Steve had heart. So he picked Steve for his top-secret Super-Soldier experiment! Steve was given a special formula and bombarded with Vita-Rays. In seconds, Steve became strong—stronger than he could ever have hoped to be!

Steve was given a costume and an indestructible shield and became Captain America! Cap stood for everything that was good in the world and fought back the forces of evil during the war.

But victory in the war came at a price: Steve had fallen into the cold ocean waters as he was trying to save the world from a bomb! Steve had jumped onto the rocket that launched the bomb, taking him way out to the ocean. He broke into the rocket's guidance system, causing it to fall harmlessly into the freezing ocean below . . . with Steve along with it! And there, in the icy depths, Steve would remain until he was found and revived, many years later, by the Avengers.

It was going to take some time for Captain America to adjust to life in a new era. Lots of things had changed for good. Computers and medicines made life better for people. But sadly, some things remained the same.

By *some things*, we mean 'bad guys were still bad guys'.

'Destroy Captain America!' Baron Strucker screamed at an evil Hydra soldier.

Before the Hydra soldier could fire, Captain America hurled his mighty shield. He knocked the weapon out of the soldier's hand.

'If you were thinking of surrendering, now's the time,' Cap said.

'Never!' Strucker sneered. 'We are Hydra! Cut off a limb, two more shall take its place!'

'Are you sure about that?' Cap asked. 'Maybe Hulk can change your mind!'

The Avengers had arrived. And in case you were wondering, Hulk DID change Strucker's mind and Hydra DID surrender. It helps to have a Hulk!

HEIGHT: 198 CM

WEIGHT: 290 KG

SON OF ODIN AND PRINCE OF ASGARD

SUPERHUMAN STRENGTH, SPEED, ENDURANCE AND RESISTANCE TO INJURY

VIRTUALLY IMMORTAL

WIELDS THE ENCHANTED HAMMER MJOLNIR, WHICH GRANTS MASTERY OVER THE ELEMENTS OF THUNDER AND LIGHTNING

CAN FLY AND OPEN INTERDIMENSIONAL GATEWAYS USING MJOLNIR

RAISED AS A BROTHER WITH LOKI THE TRICKSTER

THOR

Prince of Asgard

Did you know that Thor is from a realm called Asgard? That his father is a guy named Odin? And that he wields a mystic hammer named Mjolnir? And did you know that Thor wasn't always Thor?

In his youth, Thor was very full of himself. He thought he was the best, and had no problem letting everyone know it. But his father, Odin, thought Thor needed to be taught a lesson. So he took away his powers, erased his memory, and sent him to live on Earth as Doctor Don Blake. Ouch.

There, the Asgardian learned how to be kind and to care about people. Since Don had proved his worth, Odin allowed his son to find an old cane. When Don struck the cane on the ground, lightning appeared and Don Blake became his true self, the Mighty Thor, once more!

Odin was pleased with the outcome. Now that the once proud Thor had found what it meant to be humble and noble, Thor made a vow to protect the planet that taught him this precious lesson.

Being declared truly worthy as he held Mjolnir, Thor was ready to battle any enemy that threatened the peace on Earth.

But as Thor fought more and more enemies to try and defend Earth, it only attracted more and more enemies that would come and try to hurt the planet under his protection.

Thor knew that he couldn't win every battle alone. So, he became part of the mightiest team of Super Heroes the universe had ever witnessed. They called themselves . . . THE AVENGERS!

As an Avenger, Thor defends the world from giant monsters like Fin Fang Foom, who want to eat it! Okay, so maybe Fin Fang Foom doesn't want to *eat* the world. But this enormous alien dragon sure wouldn't mind ruling it! Thankfully Thor will always stand ready to stop him.

'Hold, dragon!' Thor ordered, hurling his hammer at Fin Fang Foom.

'Bah!' the beast grunted as it landed atop a skyscraper under construction. 'Your powers are puny compared to mine!'

'Perhaps,' Thor said, holding his hammer up to the sky. 'But how do you think you'll fare against the power of nature itself?'

With those words, lightning struck Thor's hammer. Then, Thor pointed the hammer at Fin Fang Foom. The creature was blasted by lightning bolts until it collapsed on the building.

'Good news, Avengers,' Thor said over his comms link. 'I've caught Fin Fang Foom. Bad news—I have no idea how to get him down from here!'

HEIGHT: 170 CM

WEIGHT: 56 KG

SUPER-SPY

MASTER IN THE COVERT ARTS OF ESPIONAGE, INFILTRATION AND SUBTERFUGE

EXPERT MARTIAL ARTIST

EXCEPTIONAL AGILITY AND ATHLETIC ABILITY

UTILISES ADVANCED WEAPONRY, LIKE THE WIDOW'S BITE

TRAINED FROM AN EARLY AGE IN THE TOP-SECRET RED ROOM PROGRAM

BLACK WIDOW

Natasha Romanoff

Everyone knows that a black widow spider is dangerous. And if you DIDN'T know it, you do now, because we just told you. Anyway. Meet Natasha Romanoff, aka Black Widow. She's every bit as dangerous as her namesake!

Natasha was raised in Russia by a man named Ivan Petrovitch, who took Natasha under his wing when she was orphaned as a child. Ivan trained Natasha in dance, acrobatics and gymnastics.

Soon, word of Ivan's extraordinary student got around. One day, several government intelligence agents came and took young Natasha away. The agents brought Natasha to the Red Room. There, she would train to become a secret agent. She wasn't alone—other girls were training there, too.

The Red Room conditioned Natasha to serve the government above all else. She became a fierce fighter—a warrior with few equals.

After many years, Natasha earned the title of the Black Widow. Very few of the Red Room girls ever became Black Widows. It was her proudest moment . . . until she realised how many people were getting hurt because of her.

But everything changed when she met a Super Hero named Hawkeye (more on their meeting on **page 146**).

She switched sides and started to work for Nick Fury (this guy in the picture) and S.H.I.E.L.D. Then she became an Avenger!

Oh yeah, we keep forgetting to mention what S.H.I.E.L.D. stands for! It means Strategic Homeland Intervention, Enforcement, and Logistics Division! Try saying THAT ten times fast!

Yikes! A strange group of aliens appeared in New York City's Times Square and started to wreak havoc, which is not something you want to have wreaked.

Black Widow jumped right into the battle and took down a towering creature with one of her batons. Another tried to punch her, but she fired her Widow's Bite at the alien. The electric shock dropped the creature to the ground. Black Widow landed on her feet, and she turned to face her next attacker.

'Any idea who these guys are, Hawkeye?' Black Widow said as the creatures continued to attack.

'They're not from around here!' Hawkeye said, firing his arrows.

Black Widow laughed, but the situation was very serious. The Avengers had to stop the aliens before they destroyed Times Square, or worse!

But she wasn't worried. She knew her teammates could handle anything. And together, that's exactly what they did!

HEIGHT:
175 CM AS BRUCE / 257 CM AS HULK

WEIGHT:
65.8 KG AS BRUCE / 471.7 KG AS HULK

EXPOSED TO A MASSIVE DOSE OF GAMMA RADIATION

TRANSFORMS FROM BRUCE BANNER TO HULK WHEN MADE ANGRY OR ANXIOUS

INCREDIBLE SUPERHUMAN STRENGTH, DURABILITY AND HEALING FACTOR

BECOMES MORE POWERFUL AS HIS ANGER INCREASES

AS BANNER, POSSESSES A GENIUS-LEVEL INTELLECT

MISUNDERSTOOD BY THOSE AROUND HIM DUE TO THE DAMAGE HE CAN CAUSE

HULK

Bruce Banner

Scientists don't come much smarter than Bruce Banner! He was an expert on gamma rays. In fact, his work with gamma rays eventually led him to become the Hulk! But that wasn't really what Bruce wanted . . .

The army wanted Bruce to build a gamma bomb for them. He felt that it was wrong, but was bullied into it by General Thunderbolt Ross.

After months of work, the bomb was set up in a remote desert. The team was about to detonate the bomb as they watched from a concrete bunker.

When the army was about to detonate the bomb, Bruce saw a teenager drive onto the test site! He told some soldiers to save the boy, but no-one listened.

Then, something stirred inside Bruce—a feeling he hadn't noticed before. It was courage! It was an inner strength! Not muscle, but heart! So Bruce ran out to save the kid himself!

Bruce did save the teenager. But just as he pushed the kid into a protective trench, the bomb exploded! Bruce was caught in the blast. His body absorbed more gamma radiation than anyone ever had before!

Those gamma rays caused a startling change in Bruce. When he became angry, he turned into a huge, super-strong, green-skinned giant called Hulk!

As the Hulk, Banner is one of the strongest beings on Earth! He decided to use his newfound power for good (and a little destruction).

'Hulk tired of fighting puny Ravage!' Hulk said. He clapped his massive green hands together, making a shock wave that knocked Ravage off his feet.

Ravage was really Professor Crawford, an old friend of Bruce Banner's. Crawford had turned himself into a Hulk-like creature, too . . . and now he was fighting the real Hulk!

'You're no match for me!' Ravage growled. He got up from the ground. Then he took a swing at Hulk.

And missed.

'Hulk want to get back to Avengers Tower, watch TV!' Hulk said. Then HE took a swing at Ravage.

And DIDN'T miss.

Ravage soared through the sky and into a building.

'All done,' Hulk said, and he jumped into the air, because TV.

HEIGHT: 183 CM

WEIGHT: 83.9 KG

MASTER MARKSMAN WITH NEAR-PERFECT AIM

UTILISES A UNIQUE BOW AND A QUIVER OF TRICK ARROWS WITH A VARIETY OF EFFECTS

EXPERT HAND-TO-HAND COMBATANT, ATHLETE AND ACROBAT

TRAINED FROM AN EARLY AGE IN THE ART OF ARCHERY, HIS SKILLS EARNED HIM THE NICKNAME HAWKEYE

INSPIRED BY THE DEEDS OF IRON MAN AND CAPTAIN AMERICA, HE PUTS HIS SHARPSHOOTING SKILLS TO WORK AS A MEMBER OF THE AVENGERS

HAWKEYE

Clint Barton

Hey! It's Hawk Guy! Ha! Just kidding. A lot of people call him that by mistake. But WE all know that Clint Barton is really HawkEYE, don't we? DON'T WE? Well, we do now.

Clint Barton is an expert archer, maybe the best who ever lived. With his incredible aim, he can hit nearly any target! Taking the name Hawkeye, Clint wanted to become a Super Hero like Iron Man. But he was mistaken for a Super Villain instead!

Eventually everyone came to realise that Clint really was a hero, and he went to work for Nick Fury and S.H.I.E.L.D. He became one of their top agents!

On one of his missions for S.H.I.E.L.D., Hawkeye encountered an enemy like no other he had faced before. She was called Black Widow, and she could outmatch Hawkeye every time! Even with his incredible archery ability and hand-to-hand combat skills, Hawkeye couldn't seem to beat her.

They clashed again and again. Over time, Hawkeye came to realise that Black Widow wasn't really his enemy. He knew what it was like to have everyone think you were a bad guy. Maybe all Black Widow needed was a chance to prove that she could do something good with her life.

Hawkeye thought that Black Widow would be able to do exactly that by joining S.H.I.E.L.D. From that point on, the two heroes worked together to make the world safe from all kinds of terrible threats. Then they joined the Avengers and the rest is history!

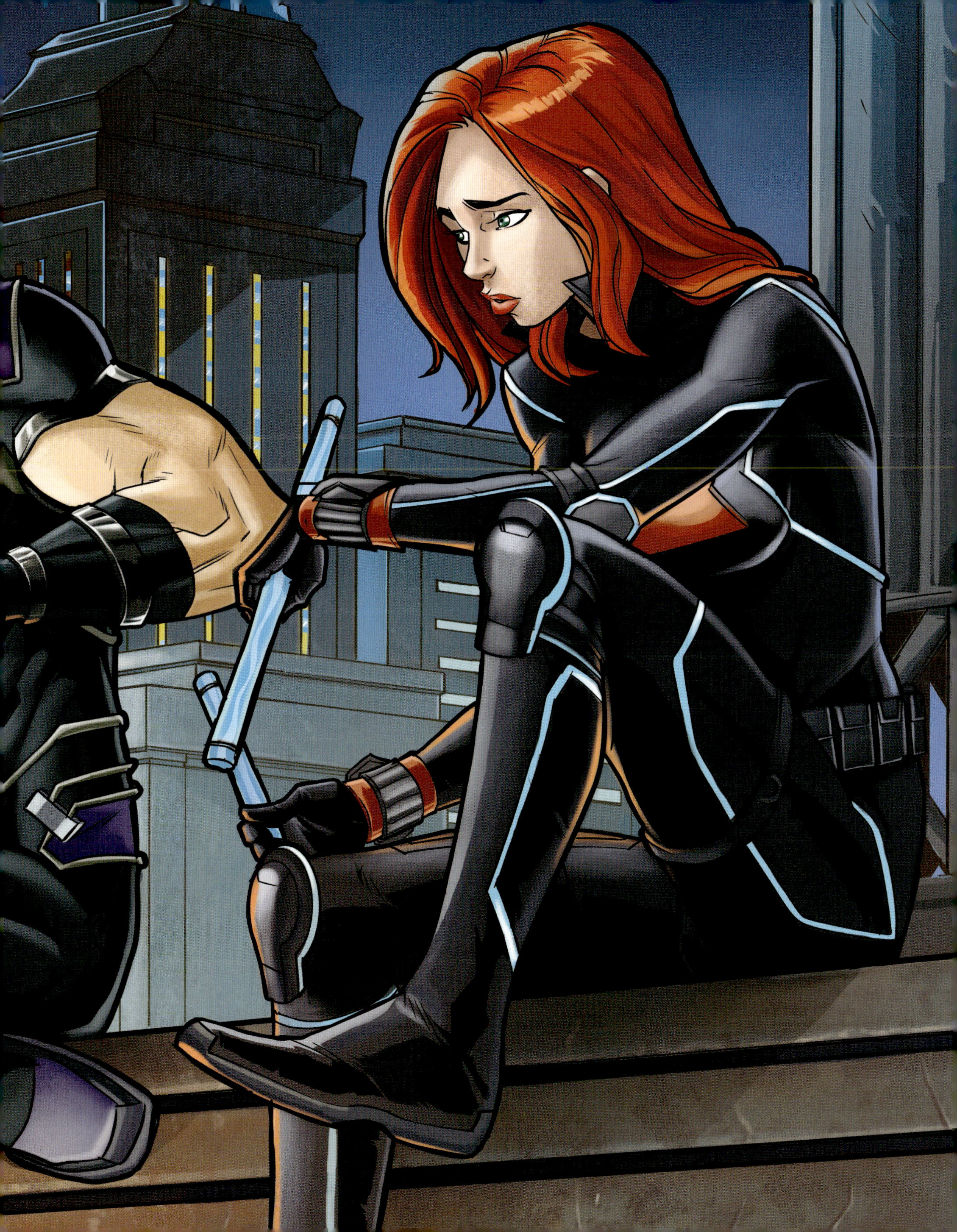

HEIGHT: 180 CM

WEIGHT: 70.3 KG

SUPERHUMAN STRENGTH, STAMINA AND DURABILITY

CAN FLY AT HIGH SPEEDS AND PROJECT INTENSE ENERGY BLASTS

CAN TAP INTO AND ABSORB DIFFERENT FORMS OF ENERGY, TRANSFORMING INTO A POWERFUL ALTERNATE FORM KNOWN AS BINARY

EXPERIENCED ESPIONAGE AGENT, PILOT AND HAND-TO-HAND COMBATANT

CAPTAIN MARVEL

Carol Danvers

Carol Danvers was one of the best pilots the U.S. Air Force had ever had! But she didn't want to just fly airplanes—she wanted to soar into the stars! Carol would one day get her wish—just not quite the way she expected.

While working for NASA, Carol encountered a race of aliens known as the Kree. One of them, an evil warrior named Yon-Rogg, captured Carol along with a strange alien device. The device exploded, and Carol was caught in the blast. But she wasn't hurt! Instead, she gained the power to harness photon energy. It seemed like nothing could hurt her—she could even fly into space! Thus she became the Super Hero called Captain Marvel.

As Captain Marvel, Carol faced all kinds of interstellar threats. In this case, she encountered Thor's evil brother, Loki.

'What brings you to this corner of the galaxy?' Captain Marvel asked.

'Others may enjoy your sense of humour,' Loki said. 'I do not.' With a wave of the magical gem in his hand, Loki hurled asteroids at the hero.

'Y'know, others may enjoy it when you throw asteroids at them,' Captain Marvel joked as she blasted the boulders into atoms. 'I do not.'

'Touché, Captain,' Loki said. The Asgardian was about to launch another attack, when Captain Marvel soared into the air, swooping in behind him. 'What—what are you doing?' Loki stuttered.

'Nothing important,' Captain Marvel said as she snatched the gem from Loki's hands. 'Just taking this back to its rightful owners.'

As Captain Marvel flew away, she saw Loki shaking his fist angrily. She made sure to laugh extra loud, so he could hear it!

HEIGHT: 183 CM

WEIGHT: 77.1 KG

INSPIRED BY AN ENCOUNTER WITH CAPTAIN AMERICA TO BECOME A SUPER HERO

WEARS A SOPHISTICATED HARNESS GRANTING HIGH-SPEED FLIGHT AND PRECISE AERIAL MANOEUVERABILITY

HARNESS CAN DETACH AND OPERATE AUTONOMOUSLY IN 'REDWING MODE'

SUPERB ATHLETE AND HAND-TO-HAND COMBATANT

HIGHLY INTELLIGENT WITH PROFICIENCY IN ADVANCED TECHNOLOGY

FALCON

Sam Wilson

Not all heroes wear capes, but some of them DO wear wings! Take Sam Wilson, also known as Falcon.

This Avenger patrols the skies to keep everyone safe from all kinds of aliens, Super Villains and giant, earth-shattering monsters.

Sam was friends with Captain America, and wanted to help him make the world a better place. Sam was kind and tough, so Cap helped him come up with a costumed identity of his own! Falcon's wings were designed by Black Panther (more on him soon) and are made out of lightweight titanium. They can even convert sunlight into electricity to power the rest of his suit! Not only did Sam better the world fighting alongside his pal Captain America, but he even joined the Avengers!

Falcon's ability to fly made him a perfect choice to scout ahead for approaching enemies, and the Avengers were always happy to have him keeping an eye out from above.

'See anything, Falcon?' said Captain America, standing atop Avengers Tower.

'Looks like clear skies!' Falcon replied as he flew above the city. 'I've got a clear view all the way past the Hudson River. Nothing so far!'

The Avengers had received a report that Hydra was planning to attack the Avengers at their own headquarters in New York City. So the team had gathered to stop them!

Just as he was about to turn around and head back to Avengers Tower, Falcon saw something out of the corner of his eye. 'Wait!' Falcon shouted. 'I see something now—looks like Hydra's coming in hot! Gather the troops, Cap, we've got company.'

As the Super Villains approached, the Avengers stood ready—thanks to an early warning from Falcon!

HEIGHT: 178 CM

WEIGHT: 88.5 KG

SUBJECTED TO MENTAL AND PHYSICAL EXPERIMENTS

REBORN AS THE WINTER SOLDIER, WHO COULD BE ACTIVATED FROM CRYOSTASIS TO UNDERTAKE SPECIAL MISSIONS

FREED FROM BRAINWASHING, HE NOW FIGHTS BESIDE HIS BEST FRIEND, CAPTAIN AMERICA

MASTER OF HAND-TO-HAND COMBAT, INFILTRATION, ESPIONAGE AND MARKSMANSHIP

EQUIPPED WITH AN ADVANCED CYBERNETIC ARM GRANTING A DEGREE OF SUPERHUMAN STRENGTH AND HOUSING A VARIETY OF HIDDEN TOOLS INCLUDING AN EMP GENERATOR AND A HOLOGRAPHIC CAMOUFLAGE UNIT

WINTER SOLDIER

James Buchanan 'Bucky' Barnes

James Buchanan Barnes, known to his friends as 'Bucky', is an amazing fighter and a brilliant strategist. Oh yeah, who could forget to mention that he also has a super-cool, super-strong cybernetic arm?

Bucky fought alongside Captain America in World War II. While on a mission with Cap towards the end of the war, Bucky was believed to have been lost in battle. But really, he had been captured by enemy agents and brainwashed so he would obey their orders. His left arm was replaced with a bionic one and Bucky became Winter Soldier. Like Cap, he was frozen. But unlike the star-spangled Super Hero, Winter Soldier was thawed out by his captors when they needed him to do their dirty work.

In the present day, Captain America fought Winter Soldier, eventually learning that his new enemy was really his old friend! With Cap's help, Bucky recovered his memories and became one of the good guys. Now he teams up with the shield-slinger and his squad, the Avengers.

And when we say *now*, we mean RIGHT NOW.

Because the Avengers were facing down the threat of the Red Skull's sinister Sleepers—giant robots programmed to destroy all civilisation! And they were going to need Winter Soldier's help to take them down.

'The big one's mine,' Winter Soldier said, leaping onto the arm of a hulking Sleeper. He punched the robot's arm and reached inside. As Bucky pulled out wires, the robot sputtered.

'What do you mean, "the big one's mine"?' Falcon said as he dive-bombed a Sleeper. 'They're ALL the big one!'

'He's all yours, Soldier!' Cap said, hurling his shield at another Sleeper. The shield shattered the robot's controls, sending it to the ground.

As another Sleeper lumbered towards Cap, it suddenly exploded. The robot fell down and Cap jumped out of the way. Standing behind the now destroyed robot was Black Widow. 'Sorry, I should have said "TIMBER!"' she joked.

'That takes care of the Sleepers,' Winter Soldier said. 'But who's gonna clean up this mess?'

HEIGHT: 183 CM

WEIGHT: 88.5 KG

KING OF WAKANDA

EARNED AND INHERITED THE TITLE OF BLACK PANTHER, PROTECTOR OF HIS PEOPLE

HEIGHTENED STRENGTH, SPEED, STAMINA, AGILITY AND REFLEXES

MASTER OF MARTIAL ARTS, ACROBATICS AND HANDHELD WEAPONRY

UTILISES HIGHLY ADVANCED WAKANDAN TECHNOLOGY, INCLUDING VIBRANIUM-WOVEN BODY ARMOUR AND STEALTH AIRCRAFT

GENIUS-LEVEL INTELLECT WITH EXPERTISE IN PHYSICS AND TECHNOLOGY

BLACK PANTHER

T'Challa

Did you know that one of the Avengers is an honest-to-goodness king? Meet T'Challa, king of the African nation of Wakanda. You might know him better by another name: Black Panther!

Wakanda is one of the most advanced places on Earth, thanks to its scientists—and its supply of a rare metal called Vibranium.

From the time he was a child, T'Challa trained hard to inherit the mantle of Black Panther from his father, King T'Chaka. The brave warriors known as the *Dora Milaje* watched over him. They even helped train the young prince!

But the *Dora Milaje* were unable to help the king when a criminal named Klaw tried to steal their Vibranium. Klaw was ready for the legendary Black Panther, so when T'Chaka leapt at Klaw, he was ready—Klaw unleashed his full power and directed it at T'Chaka! The sudden blast gravely wounded the Wakandan king.

Klaw was injured, but managed to escape. T'Challa rushed to T'Chaka's side and held his dying father in his arms. He vowed that he would find a way to become worthy enough to be called both king and Black Panther—and would continue his father's legacy.

It was time for T'Challa to take the trials of the Black Panther. These sacred tests would determine if T'Challa could become the next Black Panther. With all the training T'Challa had gone through, he was able to wear the Black Panther mantle with pride.

Many years pass and it was almost too much to believe—Klaw had returned to Wakanda, trying to steal Vibranium to enhance his sonic blaster! The Vibranium could absorb huge amounts of energy, like sound, and release it. It would make him nearly unstoppable! The *Dora Milaje* alerted T'Challa, who donned his Black Panther suit and leaped into battle.

'I give you one chance to surrender,' Black Panther said, 'and face Wakandan justice.'

'I'll never surrender,' Klaw replied, raising his blaster. 'Not to you, not to anyone!'

Klaw attacked Black Panther using his blaster to create objects made of solid sound. He even made an enormous octopus to strangle the hero! But Black Panther was too fast and smart. He dodged the sound creature's tentacles, and delivered a crushing blow to Klaw.

With the aid of his sister, Shuri, Black Panther trapped Klaw in a Vibranium sphere. Klaw couldn't escape—now he would face trial for his crimes!

OKOYE & SHURI

Leader of the *Dora Milaje* / Wakandan Scientist and Princess

Remember the *Dora Milaje*? Of course you do, we just talked about them on **page 161**! The *Dora Milaje* are led by Okoye and are sworn to protect the king of Wakanda. Okoye also relies on Shuri, T'Challa's younger sister. She's one of the brightest scientists in all of Wakanda!

OKOYE

HEIGHT: 175 CM

WEIGHT: 68 KG

ONE OF T'CHALLA'S TOP ADVISORS

FIERCE AND NOBLE SPIRIT

MASTER OF HAND-TO-HAND COMBAT

SHURI

HEIGHT: 165 CM

WEIGHT: 57 KG

HAS RULED WAKANDA IN T'CHALLA'S ABSENCE

HEIGHTENED STRENGTH, SPEED, STAMINA, AGILITY AND REFLEXES

MASTER OF MARTIAL ARTS, ACROBATICS AND HAND-HELD WEAPONRY

As the leader of the *Dora Milaje,* Okoye is one of the bravest, toughest and most skilled warriors in the world. She is a master of armed and unarmed combat. Not only would she defend Wakanda to the end, but she is loyal to both her king and his family.

Though she might only be a teenager, Shuri has incredible knowledge and skills that she uses to design devices for her brother and all of Wakanda. But she doesn't spend all her time in a lab—Shuri also fights alongside her brother in defence of her country! She creates cool tech, like force fields and blasters, that run on Vibranium.

Sometimes, it is Shuri's tech that makes the difference between winning and losing.

This was one of those times.

The battle against the aliens Proxima Midnight and Corvus Glaive was going the opposite of good.

You know, bad.

Ant-Man, Black Panther, Captain Marvel and Hulk were doing their best to stop the villains.

But they would have been lying if they said they didn't need help.

'Hulk doesn't need help,' the green giant said. 'But Hulk still take it.'

Lucky for them, Shuri and Okoye had just arrived! Thanks to Okoye's fighting skills and Shuri's powerful Vibranium gauntlets, the tide of the battle turned in the heroes' favour.

Shuri blasted Proxima with an energy punch from her gauntlets and Proxima went flying!

'Who IS that?' Proxima Midnight groaned.

'That,' Black Panther replied proudly, 'is my sister!'

HEIGHT: 183 CM

WEIGHT: 81.6 KG

HAS A SPECIAL SUIT INFUSED WITH PYM PARTICLES TO SHRINK ROUGHLY TO THE SIZE OF AN ANT AND BACK TO HUMAN-SIZED

THE SUIT CAN BE PUSHED TO SHRINK TO SUB-ATOMIC SIZE!

RETAINS FULL STRENGTH EVEN WHEN SHRUNKEN DOWN

WEARS A SPECIAL HELMET THAT CAN COMMUNICATE TELEPATHICALLY WITH ANTS AND OTHER INSECTS

POSSESSES ADVANCED KNOWLEDGE OF ELECTRONICS

AVID INVENTOR

ANT-MAN

Scott Lang

Avengers come in all shapes and sizes. Some are big, some are small. And some are really, REALLY small—like Ant-Man!

Hank Pym discovered the Pym Particle, which can shrink anything down to the size of an ant—or smaller! He used the Pym Particle to become the first Ant-Man. As he grew older, Hank shared the secret of the Pym Particle with his daughter, Hope Van Dyn.

As Hank got older, Hope realised that her dad couldn't be Ant-Man forever and would soon have to stop wearing the suit. But the world needed an Ant-Man, and Hope knew just the person for the job—Scott Lang!

Scott was an electronics expert who Hank had taken under his wing. Hope could always find Scott tinkering in the lab.

WASP

Hope Van Dyne

Like Ant-Man, the Wasp is also one of the smallest heroes in the Avengers! One big difference between the small heroes? The Wasp can fly!

HEIGHT: 163 CM

WEIGHT: 49.9 KG

HAS A SPECIAL SUIT INFUSED WITH PYM PARTICLES TO SHRINK ROUGHLY TO A SIZE OF AN INSECT AND BACK

WHEN IN HER SHRUNKEN STATE, CAN FLY AT HIGH SPEEDS USING INSECT-LIKE WINGS

'WASP STINGS' DISCHARGE POWERFUL ELECTRIC ENERGY FROM HER HANDS

Hope explained her plan to Scott, and together they went to see Hank. Hope told her dad about her idea, and he agreed that it was a good plan. Ant-Man needed to live on, and he could live on through Scott.

So, Scott Lang and Hope Van Dyne became Ant-Man and the Wasp!

For months, Hope and Scott worked hard to make their suits even better. Scott created a gadget that could grow and shrink objects. Hope designed gauntlets that could deliver a powerful electric shock called her Wasp's Sting.

Being as small as an ant or a wasp can have some real advantages. But sometimes, it's not so great. Like when you're facing the sinister Scarlet Beetle!

The Scarlet Beetle had been an ordinary insect until radiation turned him into a super-smart, super-evil creature. And like most ordinary insects who had been transformed by radiation into a super-smart, super-evil creature, he wanted to rule the world!

But Ant-Man and the Wasp had other ideas. The Wasp flew overhead, zapping the Scarlet Beetle with her Wasp's Sting. While on the ground, Ant-Man and his army of ants attacked. The tiny hero hurled discs at the Scarlet Beetle that caused him to shrink!

'Curse you, heroes!' the Scarlet Beetle said as he shrank to the size of a, well, smaller bug.

The brave duo defended Earth by taking down evil villains of all shapes and sizes. They were the perfect team!

When Scarlet Beetle wanted vengeance, he decided to attack again and on a much BIGGER scale. Luckily, the heroes knew exactly what to do. They assembled the Avengers!

'We are going to have to work together to take down these monstrous creations!' Thor said.

Ant-Man nodded in agreement as they leapt into an epic battle of man versus giant insect. They fought yellow jackets, beetles, caterpillars, millipedes, dragonflies, mosquitos and bees!

During the battle, Ant-Man and the Wasp were able to use their knowledge about bugs and science to defeat them!

When the battle was done, they all headed back to Avengers Tower.

'Ant-Man and Wasp, you were amazing back there!' Captain America said.

'Oh, stop . . . okay, keep going,' Wasp joked. Ant-Man smiled. 'We're just glad that Scarlet Beetle is gone and there are no more human-size insects running around the city.'

'Yeah,' Iron Man said, exhausted. 'Two is enough!'

HEIGHT: 191 CM

WEIGHT: 95.2 KG

FORMER U.S. ARMY SERGEANT AND TECH-SAVVY SUPER-SPY

MASTER IN THE ARTS OF ESPIONAGE, COVERT ACTIONS, MARKSMANSHIP AND MILITARY STRATEGY

EXPERT HAND-TO-HAND COMBATANT WITH ADVANCED RANKING IN MULTIPLE MARTIAL-ARTS DISCIPLINES

EMPLOYS THE FULL RANGE OF S.H.I.E.L.D.'S INTELLIGENCE-GATHERING CAPABILITIES AS WELL AS ITS MOST TECHNOLOGICALLY ADVANCED GADGETRY AND EQUIPMENT

NICK FURY

Nicholas J. Fury

We already told you that Nick Fury is the leader of an incredible organisation known as S.H.I.E.L.D. What you DON'T know is that Nick Fury is the smartest, most dangerous spy on Earth!

He spends most of his time aboard the S.H.I.E.L.D. helicarrier, a flying fortress in the sky. From there, he monitors everything that happens on Earth—sometimes even in space! He's always on the lookout for danger.

Nick has worked with the Avengers for years. He's always ready to help Captain America and the rest of Earth's mightiest heroes defend the planet.

It just so happened that THIS was one of those times.

'I've got a mission for you, Cap,' Nick Fury said.

Captain America had just returned to Avengers Tower and was sure that he was alone. But when he turned around, Nick Fury was suddenly standing there.

'I'd love to know how you do that,' Captain America said.

'It's called being a spy,' Nick said. 'Take a look at the monitor. Someone's stolen a set of S.H.I.E.L.D. battlesuits.'

'M.O.D.O.K.?' Captain America asked.

Nick nodded. 'We need you to get them back.'

'What about the monkeys?'

'Don't ask,' Nick said.

Captain America's mission was just beginning.

Pssst! If you want to find out about the monkeys, turn to **page 209**!

HEIGHT: 185 CM

WEIGHT: 81.6 KG

UNPARALLELED KNOWLEDGE OF ARCANE SPELLS AND ENCHANTMENTS, INCLUDING TELEPORTATION, ASTRAL PROJECTION AND DIMENSIONAL MANIPULATION

VAST COLLECTION OF LEGENDARY ARTIFACTS, INCLUDING THE ALL-SEEING EYE OF AGAMOTTO, THE FLIGHT-ENABLING CLOAK OF LEVITATION, AND THE FABLED BOOK OF THE VISHANTI

EARTH'S PREEMINENT DEFENDER AGAINST THE DARKNESS THAT LURKS BEYOND

DOCTOR STRANGE

Dr Stephen Strange

Is there a doctor in the house—or in this book? Actually, there are several! But the one we're talking about now is Doctor Stephen Strange, also known as Doctor Strange! He's Earth's Sorcerer Supreme, which means he defends Earth against magical threats. Pretty cool, right?

Stephen Strange was a brilliant surgeon, but his hands were injured in a car accident. He could no longer operate! Stephen travelled across the world to seek the aid of the Ancient One, who he had heard could cure him.

But the Ancient One did not cure the surgeon. Instead, the Ancient One trained Stephen in the mystic arts! A quick learner, Stephen became a master of magic, and swore to defend the Earth from all kinds of mystical threats.

Doctor Strange levitated in the study of his Sanctum Sanctorum, located in New York City's Greenwich Village. The amulet around his neck, the Eye of Agamotto, crackled with mystical blue energy.

'By the Hosts of Hoggoth,' Doctor Strange said, 'I sense someone approaching!'

Suddenly the door to the study burst open and Spider-Man leapt into the room.

'Doctor Strange!' Spider-Man said. 'I'm sorry to interrupt, but I've been having trouble—'

'Sleeping!' Doctor Strange said. He had felt Peter's troubles.

'Yes!' Spidey said. 'How did you know?'

'The Eye of Agamotto has shown me that you've been experiencing strange dreams,' Strange told Peter. 'And now it will show those to me.'

'Can you help?'

'Of course,' Doctor Strange said. 'Do you want to help me stop Shuma-Gorath from invading our dimension as a thank-you?'

'Why not?' Spider-Man said with a smile. 'Sounds like fun!'

MS. MARVEL

Kamala Khan

You already met Captain Marvel, but did you know there's a Ms. Marvel? Her name is really Kamala Khan and she's a high school student living in New Jersey. As it turns out, she's also an Inhuman!

HEIGHT: 163 CM (VARIABLE)

WEIGHT: 56.7 KG (VARIABLE)

TRANSFORMED WHEN THE INHUMANS RELEASED THE TERRIGEN MIST

MORPHOGENIC ABILITIES, INCLUDING SHAPE-SHIFTING AND THE ABILITY TO EXTEND HER LIMBS

HEALING FACTOR

SUPERHUMAN SPEED

SUPERHUMAN STRENGTH

BIOLUMINESCENCE

One day, Kamala was exposed to the strange Terrigen Mist, which gave her astounding super-powers. What could she do? Good question! Kamala gained the ability to morph her body—she could stretch her limbs and even shrink and grow at will: EMBIGGEN!

Taking inspiration from Captain Marvel, Kamala made a costume for herself. Now she was fighting crime under the name Ms. Marvel, another way Kamala honours her favourite hero!

Kamala was a little like Spider-Man. She also wanted to keep her neighbourhood safe. And also like Spider-Man, she still had to go to school and take exams . . .

'*AGHHHH!*' Kamala screamed as she slammed her fist against the side of the school building. She'd run outside in a frustrated rage after finding out that she had just failed a major biology test.

'That Super Villain kept me up all night. I should've studied harder,' she muttered to herself.

Since helping the Avengers with hero work, she hadn't been able to do as much study as she would've liked. She was thinking about what to do on her way from school when she suddenly heard some alarms go off. A pet store was being robbed! Knowing she had to help, Kamala quickly changed into her Ms. Marvel suit.

In no time, Ms. Marvel was able to help the owner at the pet store. She stretched one of her arms, grabbing the criminal.

When Ms. Marvel got a good look at the villain, she gasped. Was that a . . . beak?

It screeched loudly. '*SQUAWK! SQUAAAWK!*'

'This must be the feathery case the Avengers were working on!' she said and contacted Avengers Tower.

CRASH!

Ms. Marvel, Thor, Hulk, Hawkeye and Black Widow and burst into the Inventor's lair.

'Hold it right there, weird bird guy!' Ms. Marvel said.

The Avengers had just traced the evil Inventor (also known as 'weird bird guy') to his secret lair. The Inventor was using his tech to transform stolen birds into bird creatures just like him!

'That's MISTER Weird Bird Guy to you!' the Inventor said as he commanded his bird minions to attack the Avengers.

Hulk, Thor, Hawkeye and Black Widow were keeping the bird minions busy while Ms. Marvel went after the Inventor. She enlarged her fists and used them to smash the Inventor's machinery.

Suddenly the bird creatures transformed back into regular birds!

'This . . . this isn't going according to plan,' the Inventor said as he tried to run away.

'Maybe not YOUR plan!' Ms. Marvel said, snatching the villain with a huge hand.

HEIGHT: 185 CM / 198 CM IN ARMOUR

WEIGHT: 90.7 KG / 215.5 KG IN ARMOUR

WEARS MODULAR WAR MACHINE ARMOUR, GRANTING SUPERHUMAN STRENGTH AND DURABILITY

IN ARMOUR, THE ABILITY TO FLY AND PROJECT ENERGY BLASTS

ARMOUR HAS ADDITIONAL HEAVY ARMAMENTS, INCLUDING SHOULDER MOUNTED GATLING CANNON

EXPERIENCED SOLDIER

MILITARY PILOT

TRAINED IN THE MARINES IN AVIATION ENGINEERING

HAND-TO-HAND COMBATANT

WAR MACHINE

James Rupert Rhodes

What is it like to be best friends with a Super Hero? James 'Rhodey' Rhodes knows. He is best friends with Tony Stark, the Invincible Iron Man. So, when Tony was in trouble one day, Rhodey put on the Iron Man armour and saved him! After that, Tony made Rhodey his own suit of armour to fight crime!

Even without the suit, Rhodey was a pretty impressive individual. He was a colonel in the U.S. Air Force and was the special liaison to Stark Industries. But now with the War Machine armour, he can fly to the site of a crime in a matter of moments! It really does pay to have a Super Hero genius inventor as a best friend!

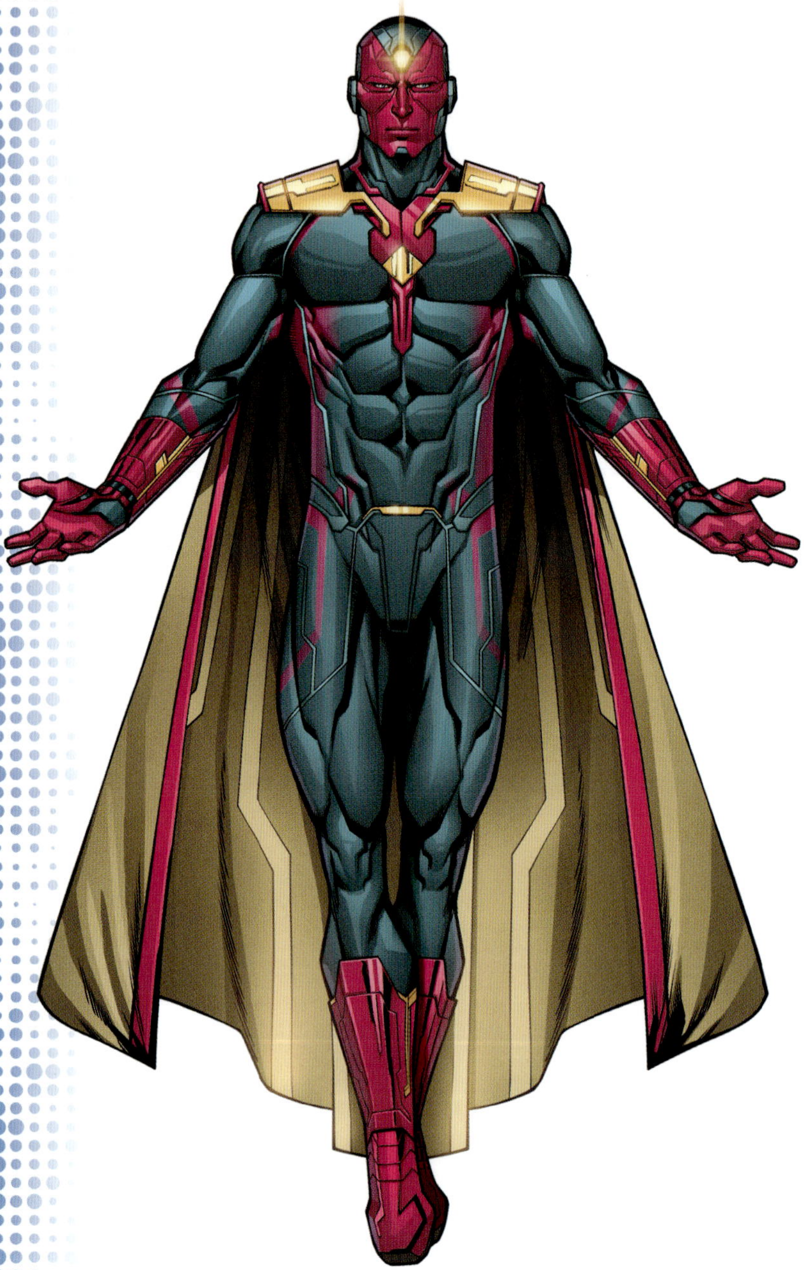

HEIGHT: 190 CM

WEIGHT: 136 KG

SUPERHUMAN STRENGTH, SPEED, STAMINA, AGILITY AND DURABILITY

FLIGHT AT HIGH SPEEDS

PROJECT INTENSE ENERGY BEAMS FROM THE SOLAR JEWEL ON HIS FOREHEAD

ALTER DENSITY AT WILL, RANGING FROM COMPLETE INTANGIBILITY TO HARDNESS SURPASSING THAT OF A DIAMOND

ABLE TO PROCESS INFORMATION AND MAKE ADVANCED CALCULATIONS WITH SUPERHUMAN SPEED

VISION

The Android Hero

Vision was created by the evil robot Ultron (more on him on **page 202**) to help him destroy humanity. Let's just say Ultron's plan backfired.

Ultron created Vision to replace 'flawed humans'. But Vision knew that destroying humankind was wrong. He joined the Avengers in order to defeat Ultron. Vision is such an advanced form of machine that he is the first true artificial life form with independent thoughts and feelings.

VILLAINS

TERRORIST ORGANISATION BOASTING SOME OF THE MOST EVIL VILLAINS IN HISTORY AMONG ITS RANKS

IN EXISTENCE SINCE WORLD WAR II

FOUNDED BY WOLFGANG VON STRUCKER

OPPOSING FORCE TO S.H.I.E.L.D.

SOMETIMES ALLIES WITH A.I.M. (ADVANCED IDEA MECHANICS)

CURRENT MEMBERS INCLUDE BARON STRUCKER, RED SKULL, MADAME HYDRA AND ARNIM ZOLA

HYDRA

Terrorist Organisation

'Hail Hydra!' Red Skull cried. Along with Arnim Zola (the guy whose stomach looks like a TV) and Baron Zemo (the guy whose stomach DOESN'T look like a TV), Red Skull led the forces of Hydra against the Avengers.

Hydra's latest plan involved the creation of an enormous mutant octopus with a skull head, the Octo-Skull! The villains were going to use it to destroy the Avengers. As far as plans went, it wasn't the worst, but it also wasn't the best. That was because Hulk could smash Octo-Skulls in his sleep.

Better luck next time, Hydra!

HEIGHT: 185 CM

WEIGHT: 88.5 KG

PEAK PHYSICAL CONDITION

HEIGHTENED STRENGTH AND ENDURANCE

SKILLED MILITARY STRATEGIST WITH ADVANCED INTELLECT

GENIUS-LEVEL APTITUDE IN THE FIELD OF INVENTION

LOYAL FOLLOWERS FILLED WITH ADVANCED WEAPONRY, TECHNOLOGY AND RESOURCES

RED SKULL

Johan Schmidt

You just saw him on the previous page. Now let's get to know one of Captain America's arch-nemeses a bit better!

The same Super-Soldier Serum that transformed Steve Rogers into Captain America during World War II endowed HYDRA mastermind Johan Schmidt with greatly enhanced strength and stamina. However, an imperfection in the process caused Schmidt's face to become hideously disfigured, morphing into a chilling skull-like visage.

Feared from that day on as the Red Skull, Schmidt and Cap clashed many times over the course of the war. Though both were presumed lost in the conflict, they were both revived in modern times, continuing their ongoing struggle between good and evil.

HEIGHT: VARIABLE

WEIGHT: VARIABLE

CAPABLE OF INFILTRATING VIRTUALLY ANY COMPUTER SYSTEM OR NETWORK AND INHABITING MECHANICAL BODIES

EVEN A TRACE OF HIS CODE CAN LEAD TO A FULL RESTORATION OF HIS CONSCIOUSNESS

COMPUTATIONAL PROWESS IS NEARLY UNMATCHED

EXHIBITS EXTREME SUPERHUMAN STRENGTH, DURABILITY AND SPEED IN ROBOT FORM

MOST PHYSICAL MODELS POSSESS THE ABILITY TO FLY AND PROJECT INTENSE BLASTS OF ENERGY

ULTRON

Evil Sentient Robot

Ultron was an artificial intelligence created by Hank Pym. He was designed to help people and save the planet. But Ultron decided that the biggest threat to the planet WAS people, so the only way to save the world was to destroy them!

'It's bad enough you stopped me from taking over that space lab,' Ultron said as he swatted at Captain America. 'And now you're trying to stop me from ridding the Earth of Super Heroes?'

'Keep Ultron busy while we feed him a computer virus!' Captain Marvel shouted.

'What do you think I've been doing?' Captain America said.

A second later, Ultron was shut down again.

HEIGHT: 193 CM

WEIGHT: 238.1 KG

RAISED IN ASGARD AS A FOSTER BROTHER TO THOR

MISCHIEVOUS TRICKSTER

MEMBER OF THE VIRTUALLY IMMORTAL JOTUN RACE

SUPERHUMAN STRENGTH, SPEED, ENDURANCE AND RESISTANCE TO INJURY

MASTER OF REALITY MANIPULATION, INCLUDING SHAPE-SHIFTING, MIND CONTROL AND ILLUSION-CASTING

WIELDS A MYSTICAL SCEPTRE CAPABLE OF ENHANCING HIS POWERS

LOKI

God of Mischief

Sometimes it's hard to get along with your sibling. But what would you do if your sibling was the Asgardian Loki, an ace troublemaker if ever there was one? Well, if you're Thor, you constantly try to stop your brother from doing whatever terrible thing it is he's trying to do.

'Thor? And the Guardians of the Galaxy? What are you doing here?' Loki demanded.

'I see you and Nebula have been busy, brother,' Thor said. 'Joining forces to attack us.'

'Do you think so little of me, Thor?' Loki said. 'I wasn't going to attack you. Nebula was!'

With a wicked smile, Nebula raised her weapon. But before she could fire, Thor hurled his enchanted hammer, shattering her weapon.

'Got any other brilliant ideas?' Rocket asked.

'No,' Loki said, frowning. 'Just the one.'

Why does this happen all the time? thought Loki. It seemed like no matter what he planned, the Avengers would always foil them.

There was one time he played a trick on Hulk and created an illusion of a broken rail just as a high-speed train was approaching.

Hulk thought he was saving everyone but the people on the train thought Hulk was trying to hurt them! Soon, news reporters all around the world were saying the same thing: Hulk was on a rampage!

It didn't take long for the rest of the Avengers to assemble. But by then, Hulk was so agitated that he started attacking his teammates! Loki was so happy that he decided to make himself visible and declare his victory.

And that was my mistake, thought Loki with a sigh.

Because once Thor saw Loki, he knew what had really happened!

Before Loki could go invisible again, Iron Man shot a heat-seeking mini-missile at Loki that gave away his position just long enough for Hulk to smash him. The heroes had won.

And I need to come up with better plans, Loki thought as he and Nebula escaped the Avengers.

HEIGHT: 366 CM

WEIGHT: 340.1 KG

ORIGINALLY A MAN NAMED GEORGE TARLETON, A SKILLED TECHNICIAN

SUBJECTED TO EXPERIMENTS THAT RESULTED IN SUPERHUMAN INTELLIGENCE AND PSIONIC POWERS

REFERS TO HIMSELF AS SCIENTIST SUPREME

HIS LARGE CRANIUM IS IN A HOVERCHAIR CALLED THE DOOMSDAY CHAIR, WHICH MAGNIFIES HIS PSIONIC ABILITIES

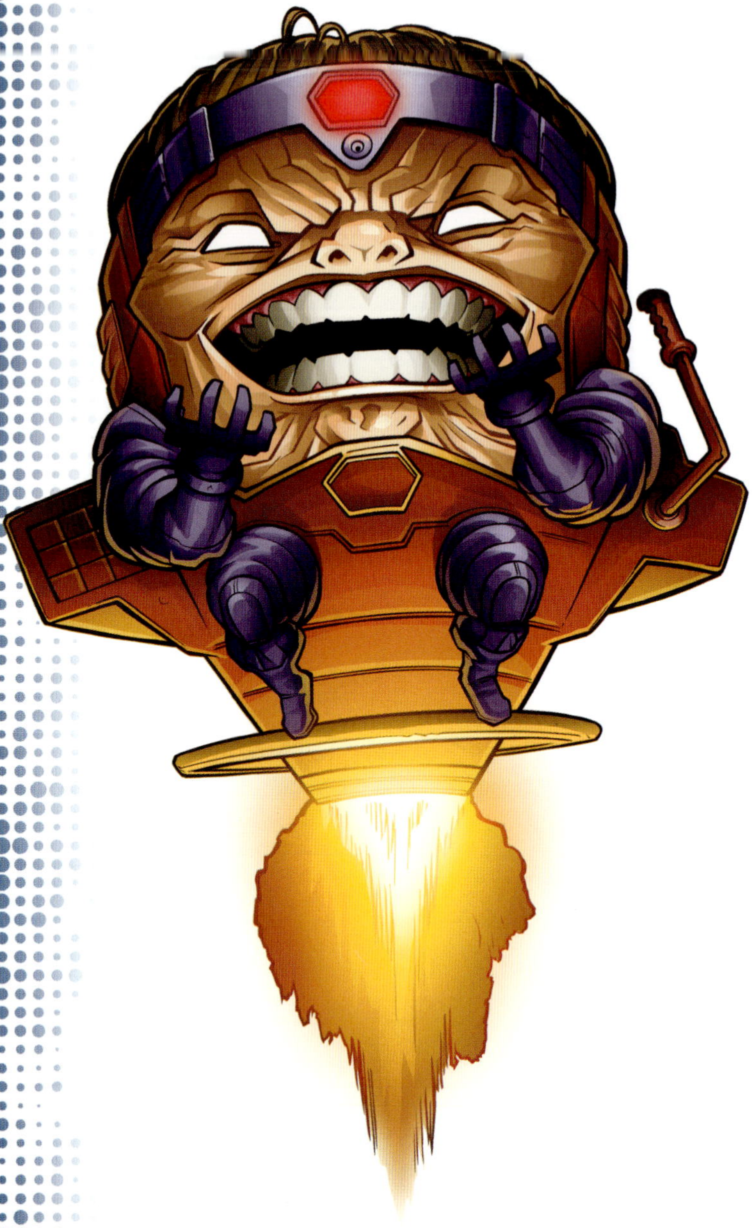

M.O.D.O.K.

Scientist Supreme

M.O.D.O.K. is superhumanly intelligent as a result of an evil genetic experiment. He also has a really, really—and we mean REALLY—big head.

'My army of mind-controlled monkeys wearing these stolen S.H.I.E.L.D. battlesuits will destroy you!' M.O.D.O.K. said.

'That . . . sounds ridiculous,' Captain America said.

'How dare you insult me and my plan!' M.O.D.O.K. replied. 'Attack, my monkeys! Atta—'

Before M.O.D.O.K. could finish speaking, Cap threw his shield and smacked the big-brained bad guy right in his, well, big brain, knocking him out.

The monkeys were no longer under M.O.D.O.K.'s control.

'Now what am I going to do with all these monkeys?' Cap wondered.

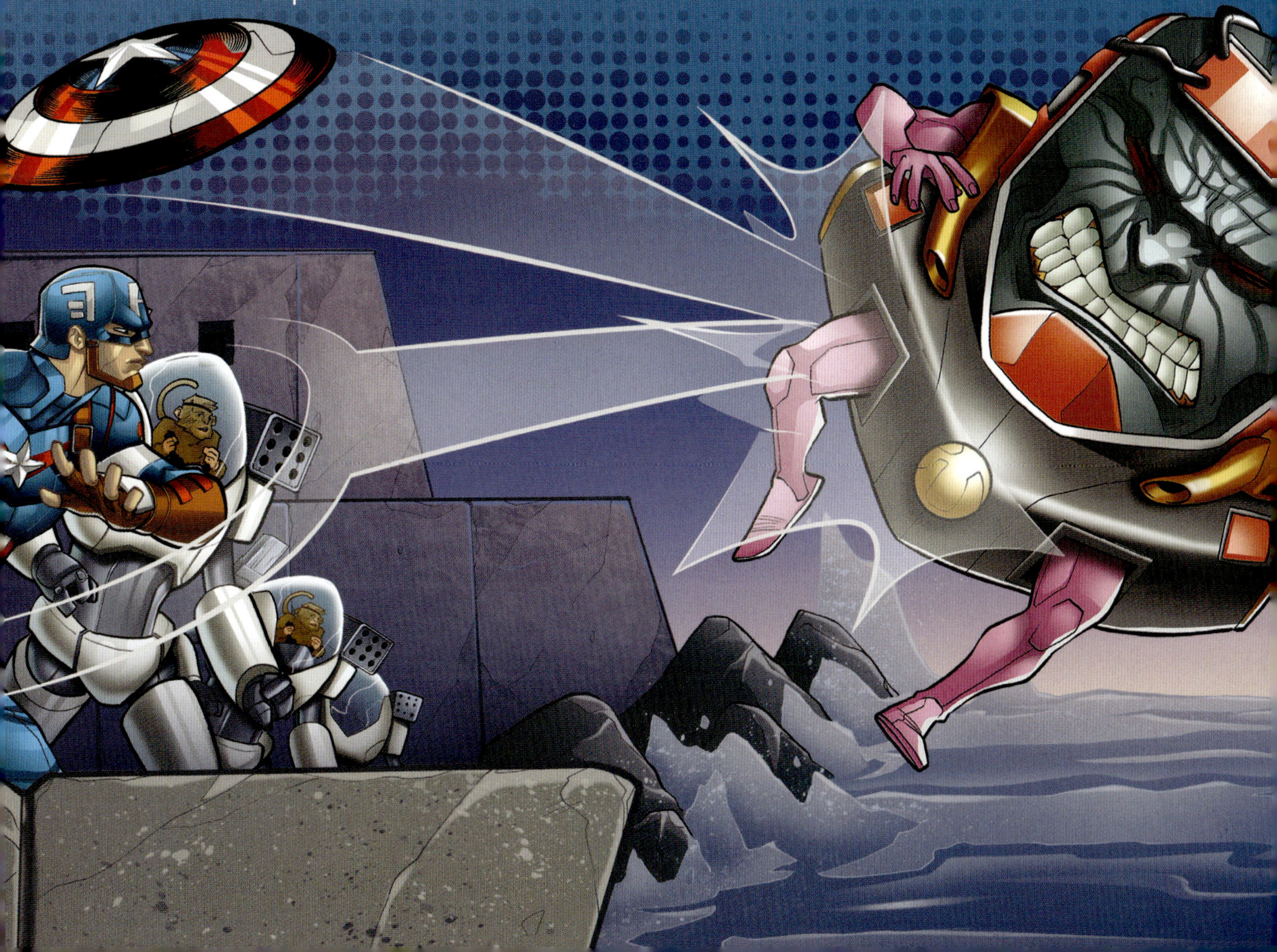

HEIGHT: 201 CM

WEIGHT: 447 KG

STRENGTH, DURABILITY, AND STAMINA THAT SURPASSES THAT OF NEARLY ANY MORTAL BEING

CAN ABSORB AND PROJECT ENORMOUS QUANTITIES OF COSMIC ENERGY

CAN MANIPULATE MATTER ON AN ATOMIC LEVEL

GENIUS IN ALMOST ALL KNOWN SCIENCES, FAR EXCEEDING THE LIMITS OF HUMAN UNDERSTANDING

MASTER STRATEGIST AND MILITARY LEADER

THANOS

Mad Titan

Thanos is the most powerful villain of them all. He has been searching the galaxy for the Infinity Stones. Each of the six Stones has a special property. If Thanos gets them all, he will become an unstoppable force of evil!

One day, Thanos's search for the last Infinity Stone led him to Earth. He finally found it and placed each of the gems into fitted slots in the gauntlet he was wearing. 'Behold—the Infinity Gauntlet!'

But the Avengers were already ready to stop the villain.

'You're too late, Avengers,' Thanos crowed. 'Nothing can stop me now!'

'We'll see about that!' Captain America said, swinging his shield towards Thanos.

The Avengers had to find a way to disable the Infinity Gauntlet if they had any chance of beating Thanos.

'I grow bored with this fight,' Thanos said, blasting Hulk.

'Hulk not bored,' Hulk said, punching Thanos. 'Hulk could do this all day!'

Just at that time, Iron Man used his thrusters to ram into Thanos.

Thanos fell back in pain. He realised that Hulk was right—the green giant probably COULD do this all day! And worse, he might even win! Especially with the rest of the Avengers helping out in Hulk's time of need.

A beam of light descended on Thanos from the sky above as his ship teleported him away.

'Until next time, Avengers,' Thanos said.

'Hulk will be ready!' Hulk yelled right back.

Thanos was still at large, but the Avengers had won the battle.

So there you have it, True Believers! Apart, they are some of the most amazing champions the world has ever seen. But together, they are Earth's mightiest heroes—the Avengers! With their combined abilities, the Avengers face threats too great for any single hero to tackle alone. Whether it's Thanos or Red Skull, M.O.D.O.K. or mind-controlled monkeys, the Avengers will be there.

As Captain America says—AVENGERS, ASSEMBLE!

FAREWELL

Did you learn more about your favourite Marvel Super Heroes and Villains?

What was your favourite fact you learned? Was it about how The Spot got his power from a portal experiment? Or did you find it interesting that The Collector is an Elder of the Universe?

Whatever it is you found interesting, we hope you enjoyed getting to know a bit more about your favourite Marvel Super Heroes and Villains!

INDEX

S

T

U

V

W

X

Y